MW00909745

Playing God

Micheline Collins

I love you so much!! Good luck Eliza! ♡M

To my family, especially my parents and my sister, and my close friends (you know who you are) for assisting my on this journey even when I felt like it would never end and to everyone I've ever known, or even merely seen or read about, for without you this book would be nothing at all.

Author's Note

There is a feeling of possession that I sometimes experience when a new character enters my head for the first time. It occurs primarily when I'm alone, often when I am walking my dog and so speaking out loud to myself seems strange to those around me, yet I do it still. One moment I will be thinking about myself or something that I need to get done and all of a sudden, I am telling a story, someone else's story, that I've felt a need to get out of my head and into the open air.

Mary Ellis, one of the protagonists of Playing God, crept into my head during a moment of possession. I had been tasked with writing a short story from a child's perspective during my fiction class and had felt largely uninspired, imagining children's lives as either completely dull or so full of tragedy that it becomes almost funny to read. But suddenly Mary Ellis was there, telling me about how her grandmother had just died and now she was packing up her life and moving to Florida and taking the whole situation in stride, not falling to pieces because of it.

I went home and began to write, and soon 'Playing God' was a short story that consisted primarily of the events of the first two chapters of this novel. It focused entirely on Mary Ellis as somewhat more brash character who believed she was partially responsible for her grandmother's death, which was the central conflict of the story. After it was finished and revised as a short story, the project completed, I set it aside to move on to the next thing I had to write for fiction class, forgetting about it almost completely in the next couple of months as I wrote more and more.

When we were tasked with writing the first thirty pages of a novel for a project at the end of the year though, my mind kept wandering back to Mary Ellis. Did she ever make it to Florida? What was waiting for her there? Did it compare to what she left behind in Pennsylvania? Even as I wrote the first thirty pages for fiction class I knew I wanted to know more, to go farther. I wanted to uncover Mary Ellis's full story and the stories of those she ended up leaving behind. So I pitched the idea for our senior thesis project, when we were required to write a full length piece. It was accepted and 'Playing God' the short story turned into *Playing God* the novel and the story of Mary Ellis turned into the stories of Mary Ellis and her best friend, Stacy, and I got the chance to tell the full story of the little girl who leapt into my head one day. I can only hope that I did it justice.

Chapter One

Five hours before everything imploded, Mary Ellis called Tommy Schwartz a "shit-faced idiot." She and her best friend, Stacy Foster, were standing on the edge of the woods, just a few steps away from where they were supposed to be playing, on Parkville School's rundown playground, but Mrs. Kaufman was barely watching them as a fight had broken out between two of the class's troublemakers, Ben Miller and Tommy Schwartz. Stacy was holding a handful of rocks, which she passed to Mary Ellis dutifully. Each time she received a rock, Mary Ellis flung it as far as she could into the woods, attempting to scare out some animals for them to see.

"Uh, Mary," Stacy said, "I think the fight might be over, maybe we should head back now." Stacy had a round, ruddy face and wet eyes, giving her a look of constantly being on the edge of tears, though Mary Ellis had never seen her cry.

"Stacy, we're fine. I'm sure a squirrel will pop out any minute now and then we can go back." Stacy frowned and peered back at the playground, where Mrs. Kaufman had sat the fighting boys on opposite side of a bench and was lecturing them angrily. Stacy could see Ben Miller's face contorted in an angry grimace, but Tommy Schwartz was just staring at the ground, kicking passive circles into the dirt.

All of a sudden Tommy's head shot up. He looked into Stacy's eyes, then at their teacher. Stacy could see his mouth moving quickly and then his arm raised, pointing right at Stacy and Mary Ellis.

"Mary," Stacy stammered, grabbing at Mary Ellis's sleeve, but before they could move Mrs. Kaufman turned around.

"Ms. Walker and Ms. Foster, please get over here now." Mrs. Kaufman guided the girls back to the bench, where they sat between the two boys that were already there. When Mary Ellis thought that Mrs. Kaufman had her back turned, she shoved Tommy's foot with her foot and muttered, "quit being a shitface idiot," under her breath.

Mrs. Kaufman snapped around to face them.

"Mary Ellis Walker that kind of language will not be tolerated here. I was going to let you off with just a warning, but I think I'm going to have to call your parents now."

"But... but..." Mary Ellis stammered, beginning to feel her heart thunder in her chest. She could only imagine what Gran would tell Mrs. Kaufman, putting on her sweetest voice and crooning, *well I don't know where she could have learned that from*. Mary Ellis didn't know how long she sat on that bench, not listening to Mrs. Kaufman explain why what she did was wrong, but eventually the bell rang, and the class trudged back inside.

The rest of the day passed quickly as Mary Ellis was unable to pay attention, her head swimming at the thoughts of the punishment she would face later that night. As she walked home from school that day she could barely hear the cars passing by, having to leap out of the way of a truck as she tried to cross the street. Even when she sat down at her dining room table, spreading her books and papers everywhere, she couldn't focus enough to do more than a few questions.

Because of this, Mary Ellis eventually gave up trying to finish her work and plopped herself down on the plaid sofa, which was torn in a few places and sour smelling from many years of use, to watch TV.

It was 4:50 p.m. when Mary Ellis heard the door creak open. She had been watching *Duck Tales*, her favorite show of all time, but was beginning to doze off, having already seen the episode many times before, so her heart leapt when she heard the tell-tale jangling of keys in the doorknob. *She's home early*, Mary Ellis thought as she jumped off the sofa and sprang towards the remote, hoping she could turn the TV off in time, but when the door opened before she could do this, Mary Ellis dashed upstairs to her room and flew into her bed.

"Mary Ellis Walker, you better get the fuck down here now." Gran was wheezing with effort as she hauled herself, and the grocery bags, into the house. Mary Ellis listened as Gran's footsteps carried her into the kitchen and then back into the living room. She cowered in her bed, the TV turned off.

"Mary Ellis, get down here."

Shaking, Mary Ellis stood. She grabbed her desk chair with both hands and dragged it across her bedroom floor. It made a god-awful screeching noise that usually would have stopped Mary Ellis right in her tracks, but Gran was angry and Mary Ellis knew it was her fault.

"You have thirty seconds to get your ass down here or you're not getting dinner."

Mary Ellis leaned the chair against the underside of her doorknob and crawled back into bed. She threw her thin blanket over her head and clamped her hands down over her ears. Gran's footsteps came up the stairs, booming. Mary

Ellis's doorknob shook for a moment and then the whole wall shook. Gran was pounding on the door.

"Mary Ellis," she screamed, "Mary Ellis you better get out here now."

The small painting in Mary Ellis's room clattered against the wall again and again. Mary Ellis could imagine Gran standing just outside, her face red as a tomato and her meaty fists just banging and banging. It seemed to go on forever.

And then the banging stopped. Mary Ellis listened to Gran's footsteps retreating down the stairs and into the kitchen where she heard the rustling of plastic bags. Tears swelled in Mary Ellis's eyes once again, so she pressed them shut, trying to keep the tears from coming. She couldn't. They burned as they streamed down her face.

"I hate you, Gran. I hate you and I wish that you were gone so that I could go back to my real home," Mary Ellis whispered into her bedsheets, balling her fists so hard that tiny crescent moons appeared on her palms. She could hear the sounds of Gran opening up a can of soup downstairs. Mary Ellis's stomach growled. She hadn't had lunch either; that morning she'd woken up late and didn't have time to pack it before Gran rushed her out the door.

"I hate you. I hate you." Mary Ellis spoke a little louder this time, her voice rising with the hunger in her stomach, but the tears overtook her and she hunkered down into bed, shaking slightly with fury. It couldn't have been too long before she fell asleep.

**

The next morning Mary Ellis woke up at 7:36 AM to the sound of her alarm blaring. She wasn't sure how long it had been ringing since she was supposed to have woken up half an hour ago to catch the bus. Usually, if she missed her alarm Gran would barge into her room screaming, now though, everything was suspiciously silent. She leapt out of bed; Mary Ellis had stayed locked in her room all night and she now felt that she was about to burst. She rushed to the bathroom, not even bothering to get changed before she ran. In the bathroom mirror her face looked puffy and red, so Mary Ellis washed it until she thought that she looked presentable. She then drifted back to her room to get dressed, hoping she looked okay for the day ahead.

Next, she crept down the hall to the last door in front of the stairs. Mary Ellis stood in front of the door for a long moment, a pit of dread forming in her stomach, before knocking.

"Gran, it's time to get up."

There was no response or sound of the bed heaving under Gran's weight as she stood.

"I can make breakfast if you want, but I need to get to school," Mary Ellis yelled, and then after a beat, "Please Gran, I'm sorry."

Still there was no response, so, for the first time in months, Mary Ellis reached for the doorknob and pulled the door open.

The air inside Gran's bedroom was stale and smelled slightly of cigarettes. Mary Ellis thought she had stopped smoking ages ago.

"Gran," Mary Ellis said, "Gran, wake up." She was still standing in the doorway.

"Gran!" There was no motion from the bed. Mary Ellis walked to its edge.

"Come on, this isn't funny, just get up. I need to get to school." When that got no response, Mary Ellis grabbed Gran's arm, but before she could shake it, she jerked back. Gran was stone cold.

"This isn't funny," Mary Ellis yelled. "This isn't fucking funny Gran." Mary Ellis paused for a moment, praying that this would be the thing that roused her. Preying that Gran would stand up. That she would scream at Mary Ellis.

"Come on get up. I'm sorry for swearing but this isn't funny at all." There was nothing.

Mary Ellis felt like she couldn't breathe, like she was going to be sick. She couldn't move.

"Okay," she whispered. *I hate you and I wish that you were gone.* The words flickered in her mind as she glared at Gran's alarm clock, which was lying on the opposite side of the bed, on Gran's bedside table. It said 7:52. It had red numbers that were much harsher than those on Mary Ellis's alarm clock, hers were blue.

Two minutes later Mary Ellis was still standing by the side of the bed, just staring at the clock. Her stomach practically screamed at her, but she didn't think she should leave Gran alone. For a long time Mary Ellis just stood there, staring at the body. She couldn't bear to be in the room though, so she let her mind wander to her and Gran's first meeting.

***

Pennsylvania's autumn air was cold on five-year-old Mary Ellis's bare shoulders. North Carolina barely ever seemed cold, even in winter, so she wasn't expecting to need a jacket. She wasn't even sure if she owned one. The air in Pennsylvania was also crisp and clean, a contrast so stark from the humid air of North Carolina that the first time Mary Ellis breathed it in, standing at the edge of the bus stairs just about to step off, her eyes went wide.

"Come on, Mary," cooed Ms. Price, the portly older woman who Mary Ellis had only met a few times before. The few times they had met, Ms. Price told Mary Ellis that she was going to be safe, that Ms. Price was going to protect her.

This time seemed to be different. *Pack your bags up*

Mary Ellis we're going to take a little trip and then later you're going to stay with your grandmother, isn't that exciting, you won't need to see me anymore. Now, stepping off the bus, Mary Ellis didn't feel too excited. As Ms. Price turned around to help her down, she shivered.

"Oh, I'll tell your grandmother to pick you up a jacket a little later." Ms. Price grabbed Mary Ellis's hand and dragged her across the bus terminal and out into the parking lot where a taxi was waiting. Mary Ellis had watched as Ms. Price called the taxi company on the bus.

"Wonderful," Ms. Price said, as she crossed to the other side of the car to climb into the passenger's seat. Mary Ellis clambered into the back, pulling her bag behind her. During the ride to her Gran's, Mary Ellis could barely pay attention to the voices of Ms. Price and the taxi driver, chattering in the front seat of the car. Instead, she pressed her face against the cold glass of the window and looked out. Red, yellow, and orange leaves fluttered from the trees and swirled through the air. It was unlike anything that Mary Ellis had ever seen.

It was about twenty minutes later when the taxi pulled up in front of a house. Though it would be the largest house she had ever lived in, she guessed in terms of the other houses in the neighborhood it was small. There were garden beds tilled out front, but the plants within them were so dead it looked as if someone had just stuck sticks randomly in the ground. She didn't have much time to look though before Ms. Price was pulling her out of the car and down the small concrete pathway up to the front door.

Ms. Price knocked. No one answered. She knocked again. When once again there was no answer, she pulled a file out of her purse and stared at the page for a moment and then up at the number of the house. She knocked again.

"Joyce Walker?" Ms. Price yelled, and at that moment

a car pulled into the house's driveway. A large, angry-looking woman climbed out of the car and began to lumber towards them. Gran.

"Oh, Mrs. Walker." Ms. Price spun around to face the older woman and reached out her hand. "Hello. My name is Shirley Price and I'm with social services. I was told you were informed of our coming, but-"

"I was," the woman spat, "I was just late leaving work. Come on, kid." Gran reached for the door to her home, breathing heavily, keys in hand.

"Well, I thought I could come in for just a moment to review a few things with-"

"Fine."

The door to Gran's house swung open and Mary Ellis was jostled into the living room. "I set up your room upstairs, so you can go unpack." Walking up those stairs for the first time, Mary Ellis felt all alone.

Two hours later, Gran called Mary Ellis down to get dinner. It was mac-and-cheese, orange, the boxed kind. Gran didn't sit with her to eat.

"So, you're going to be staying here," Gran said, and that was it, the dream of life going back to normal shattered. Mary Ellis nodded. "Well, I'm not going to let you just hang around, I have a list of things you're going to need to get done before I get home from work tomorrow."

"But at home I-"

"What it was like at your old place doesn't matter. You need to get over that. Life goes on."

***

So Mary Ellis tore her eyes away from Gran – Gran's body – and went downstairs to the kitchen. She pulled a box of waffles from the freezer and placed them in the toaster oven. In the still coldness of the house, Mary Ellis liked the small mechanical hum and click of the machine as it cooked her breakfast.

When the waffles were toasted she slathered them with peanut butter from the upper cabinet, she had to climb onto the counter to get it, and ate slowly, sitting in front of the TV. There was nothing on that she liked, but she watched anyway, afraid she would hear Gran's voice chastising her for not going to school that day.

After breakfast Mary Ellis placed her dish in the sink and then stared at it, unsure of what to do. Gran would have wanted her to wash her plate. It was a rule, but as Mary Ellis stood in front of the counter, she couldn't bring herself to turn on the tap and actually do it. Eventually, she just sat back down on the sofa.

She sat in silence, but her mind wandered, back to the door upstairs and back to Gran. What had happened to her? It couldn't have been Mary Ellis's fault; Mary Ellis was in her room all night. But maybe? *I hate you and I wish that you were gone.* Mary Ellis's heart began to pound. She scrambled for the remote, turning the TV louder and louder. She tried her hardest to focus on the images flitting across the screen, to hear nothing but the sounds of the TV, until it felt like her eyes were burning and her ears were going to burst. At some point she laid down on the couch. Eventually, her vision was blurry with exhaustion and the hazy images of cartoon characters she was no longer paying attention to; it was only then that the thought occurred to her. She was the reason Gran had gone away. It was all her fault.

That night it was hard to get to sleep.

***

The next morning Mary Ellis woke up with a splitting headache. She ate a peanut butter sandwich and watched TV for almost two hours, nothing was on, but the rhythmic pounding in the back of her head just refused to go away.

Mary Ellis screamed. She screamed to no one in particular, maybe Gran. Mary Ellis wanted to be cared for; she needed the aspirin Gran used to give her when she had headaches like these. Where did Gran keep them? Mary Ellis searched through the first-floor bathroom, then, when they were not there, realized that she must go check the upstairs bathroom.

As Mary Ellis began the trek upstairs, she could already detect a terrible smell. By the time she reached the top of the stairs, she could see the clusters of flies clinging to the walls, rushing out from under Gran's doorway. Mary Ellis gagged, but she needed to reach the end of the hall where the bathroom was. She rushed down the hall, staring straight ahead, then burst into the bathroom. She tore it apart, but there were no pill bottles anywhere. *They must be in Gran's room*, Mary Ellis thought. Gran's room. Mary Ellis went downstairs again. The headache would probably go away in an hour or two.

But the headache didn't go away. Mary Ellis needed those pills. What did Gran call them? Aleve. Mary Ellis needed the painkillers from Gran's bathroom. The bathroom whose only door could be found in Gran's bedroom.

Mary Ellis made it up the stairs alright, but when she reached the top she just stood staring at Gran's door. What if some part of Gran was trapped in there and when she opened the door Mary Ellis released it? What if the thing in Gran's room isn't Gran at all? Mary Ellis's heart began to beat quickly. What if whatever was in there was mad at her? Mary Ellis turned away from the door and walked back to the top of the stairs, but it felt like someone was tapping drum beats onto the back of her head. So, she turned back and slowly took the few steps to her Gran's door. She placed her hand on the doorknob. Almost without thinking, she began to turn the doorknob. The door slid open.

Immediately, the bitter stench of death filled her

nostrils. Mary Ellis sprinted from the doorway to the bathroom door without so much as glancing at Gran. She slammed the door and immediately fell to the floor, heaving onto the ground. Barely managing to crawl to the toilet, Mary Ellis vomited. Gran was... Mary Ellis couldn't find the word for it, but she knew it was her fault. The pounding in her head persisted so she reached up for the edge of the counter and stood. She looked at herself in the mirror, tangled hair and puffy face. There was a little bit of vomit on her chin; she wiped it off with a towel. Mary Ellis heard the phone ringing downstairs, but didn't rush to answer it.

The Aleve bottle was in the third drawer down; Mary Ellis took them, struggling to swallow them with a gulp of water she got from the tap. As she waited for the pills to take effect, Mary Ellis sunk to the floor, leaning against Gran's white, wooden counter. All at once she felt exhausted. Her limbs felt heavy, eyelids hanging low over her eyes, threatening to slide shut. She stared absently as the wall opposite her, its yellowing floral wallpaper peeling in places. Her eyes focused on the framed picture that Gran had hung on the wall there: a fading colored photo of Gran when she was younger, a tall, broad man standing next to her, bracing his hand on the back of the chair in which Gran sat. In Gran's lap, a small child writhed, its face contorted in a half-grimace, half-grin. Gran's only child. Mary Ellis's mother. Mary Ellis thought it was unfair. All around the house Gran hung photographs and paintings, tiny embroidered quotes, even fancy plates next to their fridge, but the picture Mary Ellis cared most about was kept here, in a room she was barely allowed to enter.

Standing, Mary Ellis reached for the photograph that hung on the wall. She removed it, holding the photo with both hands for only a moment before tucking it beneath her elbow and exiting the bathroom. At least for right now, Mary Ellis felt as if she had a purpose.

She hurried quickly through Gran's bedroom into her own. It was the first time she'd been inside since Gran went away. It was strange to see that the room had not changed since Mary Ellis had last been in it, the walls still sparse with decoration and the floor still cluttered with old homework assignments, half-finished books, and clothing that Mary Ellis was unsure if she had ever worn. She started with those first; selecting only that which would be most comfortable for her, T-shirts and shorts, perfect for the near-summer heat. They collected on her bed in tiny piles: one for tops, one for pants, then socks, underwear, her sweatshirt. She got three books from the shelf across the room: two Nancy Drew's stolen from the collection that Gran kept in the attic, left over from her own youth and one Junie B. Jones book that Stacy had given her for her birthday a few years ago, which she still hadn't read. It was probably too young for her now, but Stacy had told Mary Ellis that the main character reminded her of Mary Ellis.

She placed her backpack on the bed as well. It was truly awful: hot pink and marked with three pastel, sparkly ponies. According to Gran, Mary Ellis had once begged for the backpack, groaning and tugging her back to it each time that Gran and Mary Ellis went to get groceries, but now it seemed to jeer at Mary Ellis each time she saw it. She turned it around, so the ponies were facing away from her.

Finally, Mary Ellis crouched down next to her bed, reaching around the top bedpost, to remove a small stack of paper she kept there. In her hands, Mary Ellis held the key to it all: every card that Mary Ellis had received from her parents since she had left them when she was five. There were some birthday cards, emblazoned with phrases of empowerment or little jokes, still stuffed in their original envelops, which were now slightly worn and dirty, but her favorites where the postcards. Bold swirls of orange and yellow, contrasted with greens and blues. All advertising different cities in North Carolina, all marked with the same address.

23 N. Fisher St.

Apartment 2D

Pineville, NC 28134

Gradually communication tapered off, until postcards only arrived on her birthday, but they were all that she needed. Each contained only a brief sentiment of love, but she could get by on these and the promise that one day, when they were better, they were coming to get her and take her back home to North Carolina. Now it was time to force their hands. If Mary Ellis had no guardian they'd have to take her in.

She packed everything on the bed into her backpack, vowing that tomorrow she would go pick up the rest of the supplies that she needed from the local grocery store. Finally, Mary Ellis raided the 'Emergency Fund' that Gran kept in her closet, plugging her nose with pieces of tissue, though the smell still crept into her nostrils. Then, she went downstairs.

Before getting dinner, Mary Ellis checked the voicemails on their phone. There were three messages. Two were from the school, who had called to inform Gran that Mary Ellis hadn't been in school for the past two days and if she's sick she's going to need to bring in a note when she gets better, and the last one was from the manager at the local Kmart, Thomas Miller, calling just to make sure that Gran remembered she had a job and that she was expected to arrive on time for that job each and every day unless she called out sick, which was something she hadn't done. Mary Ellis didn't understand the last message, of course, Gran remembered that she had a job, how would she have forgotten? But no matter what it meant there was nothing that Mary Ellis could do.

When night descended on the house, Mary Ellis found it hard to focus on sleep. Her heart raced in her chest and her mind raced along with it: mentally calculating what she'd need to bring with her tomorrow and how she'd begin her journey. There was also the swirls of thrill and guilt that came with leaving. Mary Ellis was finally getting out of this house. She was finally going home.

Chapter Two

The next morning Mary Ellis raided the kitchen for things she could take with her. Despite the fact that Gran kept a wealth of boxed meals in their freezer, there were few things that Mary Ellis thought she could eat on the road. Eventually, she decided that she'd take two cans of black beans, the half loaf of white bread, and a jar of peanut butter. She placed these in a plastic bag, setting it next to the backpack that was already ready to go on the dining room table. Mary Ellis got the money that was left in Gran's purse, not wanting to break into the emergency fund for this.

Then, Mary Ellis got the green plastic credit card out of Gran's purse. Quickly, she logged into their dinosaur of a computer and began to search. She wasn't sure exactly how to buy a train ticket. She looked up "trains to North Carolina" and "busses to Pineville," but they only returned results for the Pennsylvania train stations themselves. It seemed that there wasn't any way to get right to Pineville, she'd have to find another way. After examining a map, Mary Ellis thought she found the cheapest way to get the farthest. She was going to go to D.C. Mary Ellis typed the tiny numbers on the front of the card into the boxes on the screen. Then, it was done. Her trip was confirmed and she printed the ticket out along with a map, folding them up and shoving them deep into her pocket. When Mary Ellis was finished she readied herself, slipping the backpack onto her shoulder, and left the house for the first time in three days.

***

The corner store was a stout teal building where Gran got all of their groceries. Though the aisles dwarfed Mary Ellis, she could tell that the cashier could see her, which made her squirm a little. She crept through the stores aisles collecting another loaf of bread, a liter bottle of water, a small jar of jam, and a handful of Cliff Bars. She gazed longingly at the case where they kept the ice cream, but Mary Ellis had to be mature now so she left the ice cream behind.

When she was handing the cashier the last of her things a few minutes later, she heard the bell over the door jingle.

"Mary?" a voice asked. It was Stacy Foster, her wet eyes gleaming. Mary Ellis didn't want to see Stacy, she was sure her hair looked messy and matted and she hadn't showered in days.

"Mary, where have you been?" Stacy walked quickly towards her and all of a sudden Mary Ellis felt like a deer in headlights. The cashier, having rung up her things, handed Mary Ellis the change she was owed and a plastic grocery bag.

"Uh, I was sick," Mary Ellis stammered. Stacy grabbed her hand and dragged her down an aisle.

"I'll be back in a second, Mom," Stacy called and when she and Mary Ellis were safely situated in the corner of the store she asked, "Where were you really?"

"It really doesn't matter."

"Well, when are you coming back to school?"

"Stacy I- I don't know." Mary Ellis stared at her feet.

"You don't know? We're all worried about you."

16

"Listen you can't tell anyone this, not even your mom."

"What?"

"I think I'm going back to North Carolina to find my parents."

"Mary, you're my only friend."

"And you're my only friend, but I need to go," Mary Ellis paused; she loved Stacy but it wouldn't be long until she ran out of money and then, "You could come with me."

Stacy stood in stunned silence for a moment.

"Well, Mary, I don't- I can't go. My dad would be too worried about me and, wouldn't your grandma be worried about you too?"

Mary Ellis didn't realize how much she wanted Stacy to come with her, how much she actually needed someone. "I uh-"

"Stacy, come on it's time to go now."

"Coming, Mom." Stacy hugged Mary Ellis quickly.

"See you tomorrow?" Stacy asked but turned away too quickly for Mary Ellis too respond.

Entering the house when she got home later that afternoon, Mary Ellis was struck by the smell of the house. Over the past few days she must have gotten used to the smell while living inside, but now the air in the house was thick with heat and stench. Mary Ellis needed to leave as soon as possible.

She put the whole bag into the fridge aside from a can of soup, which she made. Making her last preparations for her journey tomorrow, Mary Ellis pulled Gran's flip phone from her purse. She flicked it open, staring at the tiny screen for a moment before entering Stacy's cell number, the only phone number she had memorized. Snapping the phone shut, she tucked it into her pocket. Then, she curled up in front of the TV and watched cartoons for a while. Eventually, when cartoons turned into the news, she turned off the TV and pulled a blanket over herself. On a normal day she would have gone upstairs to her bed to sleep, but the stench of Gran's room would be worse on second floor, so she slept on the sofa now, like a guest in her own home. Just as she was beginning to doze off Mary Ellis pressed her eyes tightly together and prayed, *I hate Mr. Foster and I wish that he was gone*.

***

The next morning when Mary Ellis woke up, rubbing the crust from her eyes, she excitedly awaited the arrival of her best friend. She paced around the house, consolidating all of her things into one backpack and a plastic bag, tucking the $124 from Gran's emergency fund into the front pocket of her jeans. Mary Ellis figured this was deserving. When she was finished, Mary Ellis strode around the first floor of her house, passing from the kitchen to the living room to the dining room and back again, picking up random objects, observing them, and putting them back again. She was sure this would be the last time she would see this home and felt strangely nostalgic about it. She wasn't sure whether her time here had hurt her, but Mary Ellis knew that it had changed her. And now she was leaving it.

Mary Ellis sighed; she hoped Stacy would be there soon.

But by the time she heard a knock on the door, it was almost noon. Mary Ellis had relaxed onto the sofa, the TV blaring cartoons. Mary Ellis sprang up at the sound of the knock and rushed to the door, creeping on her tip-toes like Gran always told her to, so that if the person who wanted to come in was bad they didn't know she was inside. Still on her toes, Mary Ellis peeked into the door's peephole. The man outside was certainly not Stacy; in fact, Mary Ellis didn't recognize him. He was wearing a black polo with a tiny red K embroidered on the front. When Mary Ellis didn't answer, he knocked again.

"Joyce?" he yelled. The man was looking for Gran.

As he continued to knock, Mary Ellis backed away from the door. She knew what was at stake here, who the man would call if he found she was here alone. Walking to the sofa to pick up her things and ensuring that she didn't pass in front of any of the windows, Mary Ellis readied herself to leave. She crept towards the kitchen past the front door and the dining room table.

She passed into the kitchen and began to run towards the back door, hoping the man had gotten tired of pounding on the front door and went away. She reached the screened back door and pushed it open, careful to put her hand between the door frame and the door, so the man wouldn't hear it slap closed. Mary Ellis then took off through the small, fenced-in backyard, only stopping when she reached the fence to push her bag over top of it before clambering over it herself.

A puddle was behind the fence directly where she dropped her backpack, and though Mary Ellis had been able to leap farther out to avoid it the bottom of her backpack was now wet with mud. Swearing, Mary Ellis pulled it back onto her shoulder, assuring that the moment she was sure she was safe she would check to make sure everything inside was okay.

She walked through her neighbor's yard, mud dripping down her back, looking over her shoulder with every step she took, but the man never rounded the corner of the house to see her. As she walked, Mary Ellis quickly checked that everything she needed was with her, pulling open all of the pockets that her backpack held.

Mary Ellis walked out onto the street that ran parallel to hers, Maple St. The street was still, no cars bustling down the road or clusters of teenagers walking to the various hotspots in the area. There were only the trees rustling and a bird chirping somewhere off in the distance.

Mary Ellis shut her eyes for a moment, thinking of where she would be right now if everything had stayed the same. She would be sitting in math class, probably barely paying attention as Mrs. Kaufman droned on and on about how they needed to be practicing their times tables if they wanted to pass the quiz on Friday. Then each student in the class would have to stand up and recite one set of multiples in front of the class. No matter whether you started from the front or back of the classroom, from the left or the right, Mary Ellis always had to say twelve, which everyone knew was the hardest one. She would stand up, take a deep breath, her nerves rocking in her stomach and say, *One times twelve is twelve. Two times twelve is twenty-four. Three times twelve is thirty-six...* Even up to the last day of school, now less than a week away, Mrs. Kaufman would work them. Instead she was here, watching the trees rustle and listening to the birds chirp. Alone. In class Stacy would have been with her, nudging the back of Mary Ellis's seat as she stood up to speak, so Mary Ellis giggled just a little bit. Or passing her dumb little drawings of Mrs. Kaufman or Tommy Schwartz or Ben Miller or anyone else in the class, so that even when everything else seemed boring and dumb, they were having a laugh together. Mary Ellis knew that no matter how much she wanted Stacy to go with her, she couldn't wait around for her anymore.

Soon enough the police would find Gran, and then they would be looking for Mary Ellis too, so she hiked her backpack over her shoulder, tucked her plastic bag over her wrist, and started off down the street.

Chapter Three

Stacy Foster sat slumped in her seat in the middle of Mrs. Kaufman's fifth grade class, dread forming in her stomach. Each day as her teacher called attendance, Stacy could feel the tension in the classroom rising.

"Mary Ellis Walker," Mrs. Kaufman would say, right after Daniel Reynolds and before Jayden Wallace, and the whole class would fall silent, as if waiting for her brash voice to pipe up and say "here." But Stacy's whole class knew that Mary Ellis had not arrived at school that day or any other day for the past week.

"Mary Ellis." Mrs. Kaufman would say once more, as was customary when a student did not answer, but she had already checked absent on the class roster.

As always, there was no response to Mrs. Kaufman, and Stacy felt momentarily frozen.

"See you tomorrow?" Stacy had asked, almost begged, Mary Ellis when she last saw her, the artificial lights of the Mini-mart beaming down on her, making her skin crawl. Even when Stacy said it she knew what the answer would be. That's why she turned away, not because she didn't want Mary Ellis to stay. She wanted to tell someone this: her mother, Mrs. Kaufman, the man on the news who had told her that they found Mary Ellis's grandmother. But she had no one to tell.

In that way, the last memory she had of Mary Ellis felt almost like a dream. There was no one she could confide it in, so it was nebulous in her mind, details adding and subtracting each time Stacy remembered. At first, the air in the Minimart had seemed still and silent when she entered, but then Stacy remembered the whirring of the fan in the center of the ceiling and the hum of the freezers that stood behind them. And the glossy sheen that seemed to cover everything in the store. Everything in the store but Mary Ellis, who stood in the center of it all with her backpack slung over her shoulder and her hair looking like it had never been combed. And the sad, sad look that Mary Ellis had on her face when Stacy said "See you tomorrow?" like it was a question and turned away real quick so she didn't have to see it anymore. And the squeak of Mary Ellis's shoes that Stacy heard as she walked out of the store. And Stacy's mother saying "How was that friend of yours, Mary Ellis?" And Stacy saying, "She's good, Mom." And then Stacy would replay the memory in her mind again like it was all new.

And then it was recess. Stacy watched the other students get up from their desks for a moment, confused, just a little while ago they were all sitting down and Mrs. Kaufman was reading attendance. Stacy stood suddenly, finally grasping where everyone was going. Her chair grated across the classroom floor, calling the attention of her classmates. Stacy felt her cheeks going beet red as she imagined the way they would snicker at her later, but everyone seemed to look away rather quickly as it happened.

"Line up, behind Ben," Mrs. Kaufman said to the class, waving a finger at Ben Miller, who practically leapt across the classroom in anticipation, moving to stand in the doorway of the classroom. As the class did as they were told, Mrs. Kaufman locked eyes with Stacy, waving her over to the teacher's desk.

"You can head out to the playground, but be sure Ms. Hale knows you're out there." The class began to exit the classroom in a less than neat line. Stacy watched them for a second, but eventually swallowed hard and walked up to Mrs. Kaufman's desk. She lingered in front of the desk, standing with her legs crossed as the rest of the class walked into the hall.

"Stacy, have a seat," Mrs. Kaufman said. Stacy sat down across from Mrs. Kaufman at the desk.

"Now, I know things have been hard for you recently-"

***

Two nights ago, Stacy was in a similar situation, sitting across from her mother at the dining room table. Her father was upstairs, getting changed out of his work clothes, when they heard a knock on the door. Stacy's mother crossed the room and cracked open the door. Stacy caught a glimpse of a blue uniform. The police? The man muttered to her mother for a few minutes, her mother looking increasingly anxious with each moment. Stacy peered at them, try to read first her mother's lips, and then the officer's. Stacy knew it was probably about Mary Ellis or her grandma.

Yesterday, while her father was watching the news in the den, a story caught Stacy's attention. The newscaster spoke about a body that had been found in the neighborhood, they thought she had died of natural causes, but the issue now was that the granddaughter of the woman who was found was now missing. They flashed her picture on the screen. Mary Ellis.

"Stacy, honey," Stacy's mother placed her hand on Stacy's shoulder, "this officer was wondering if he could talk to you about Mary Ellis."

When Stacy nodded, the man took her mother's seat at the table, folding his arms together. He looked at her mother.

"Is it okay if I record this?"

"That's fine."

The man removed a small device from inside a case he had held at his side and set it on the table. He pressed one button. Then another. Then he leaned down close to the machine to read some numbers off of its faint LED screen. Then the man sat up, turning back to Stacy. He smiled. "My name is Detective Jake Martin. I'm trying to help out your friend, Mary Ellis. Your mom told me that you heard about what happened." The detective scratched the stubble on his chin and then reached out his hand; Stacy took it, shaking it only slightly.

"Yeah." Stacy felt her toes curling in her socked feet and pressed them against the floor. She knew that police had special training that could let them tell whenever you were lying. She'd learned that from another of her father's programs; now she wished she'd paid more attention to what they were looking for.

"We think that Mary Ellis might have run away and since you were really close friends with her, we were wondering if she told you anything about where she was going." The man leaned over the table slightly, staring at Stacy with sad, pitying eyes. For a moment Stacy thought he was going to reach for her hand again, but he sat back up, waiting.

Still, Stacy sat silent, her breath caught in her throat. She swallowed.

"Okay, maybe we'll start a little easier," Officer Martin said, keeping his voice low. "When was the last time you saw Mary Ellis?"

"It was last Thursday. I saw her at the Minimart with my mom." Stacy fumbled with a piece of junk mail that was sitting on the table. She read and reread the words on the front: *Green Machine Lawn Care. We are now offering services in your neighborhood. Call now at...*

"Did you guys talk?" the man asked, and Stacy let the piece of paper fall to the table top, sitting up in her seat.

For a moment, she considered what to say, reveal enough that he leaves but not too much. Stacy felt like a secret agent, and this was a mission she couldn't fail.

"Uh-huh." Just enough, but she knew more questions were coming. Stacy took a deep breath, gripping the table with one hand.

"About what?"

"I asked her why she wasn't in school and she said it didn't matter. And then I said I hoped she'd come back soon."

"Did she say anything about where she was going?"

Stacy froze, Mary Ellis's words running through her head. She wasn't sure how long it took to get to North Carolina, but she hoped that at some point Mary Ellis would call to let her know she was there, safe and sound. Then Stacy could tell Officer Martin what happened. Stacy knew if she let it slip now Mary Ellis would be mad at Stacy when she was eventually found. Mary Ellis used to talk a lot about her parents, especially her mom. She always said when her parents made enough money they would come and take her back to North Carolina with them, and maybe Stacy could come down and visit during the summer sometimes. If Stacy told on Mary Ellis, there was no doubt in Stacy's mind that she would never ever get that trip to North Carolina, and if Mary Ellis came back to town, they wouldn't talk anymore.

"No, sir," Stacy said.

"We believe that she may have purchased a train ticket heading to DC. Do you know of any reason why she would be heading there?"

"No." Stacy leaned back in her chair, a gesture she believed would convey how casually she was treating the situation, how little she knew, but she leaned back too far, nearly falling.

"Stacy, you know this is serious. Mary Ellis could be in danger and we need to find where she is as quickly as possible, anything you know could help."

Stacy let the chair clatter back to the floor and sat up straight once again.

"The more time that passes the harder it will be to find her. It's already been more than twenty-four hours and each time a day passes our likelihood of finding her is halved."

The detective's eyes met with Stacy's; he was frowning, sympathy gone from his eyes. Now, they were merely dark. Stacy nearly shivered.

"Sorry," she mumbled, locking her eyes on the table in front of her.

"Did she mention anything about her grandmother?"

"Not really. I just asked her whether her grandma would be mad at her for going and she said it didn't matter."

"Going where?"

"To... to the store. Her grandma never let her get the groceries and I thought she would be mad, but Mary Ellis told me it didn't matter."

The officer's frowned deepened. He glanced across the table to Stacy's mother, locking eyes with her. Stacy tried to avoid looking at either of them, just hoping for this moment to be over. There seemed to be a long stretch of silence before the officer spoke again.

"Can you think of anything else she said that may be of use to us? Stacy, we just want to make sure your friend is somewhere safe."

"No, no. I don't know anything else." Tears began to prick the corners of Stacy's eyes. She wiped them away with balled up fists.

"I know it's hard to think about what might have happened to your friend, but the sooner we can figure out what happened to her the sooner we can get her home, so if there's anything you can tell us it would be so important-"

"There's nothing," Stacy said too quickly.

The detective sighed.

"If you think of anything that might be able to help us just let your mom know. She'll let us know to come back so you can tell us. Alright?"

Stacy nodded and sank back into her seat, looking away from the officer and back at her mother, who was leaning in the frame of the kitchen door. He stood up and began to walk towards the door, Stacy's mother trailing behind him.

They muttered together, once again too quietly for Stacy to hear, but when they reached the door Stacy's mother loudly said, "Have a nice evening, sir."

***

Mrs. Kaufman put her hand on Stacy's forearm, causing Stacy to jolt.

"Stacy?" she asked, clearly expecting an answer to a question of some kind.

"I'm sorry, can you repeat that?" Stacy's voice felt weak.

"I wanted to make sure you were alright. I know it is close to the end of the year but you are usually an attentive student. I may need to call your parents if you don't even try to pay attention."

"Mrs. Kaufman..." Stacy's head was pounding, all she wanted to do was get up and walk out of the classroom into the fresh air.

"Mary Ellis was a close friend of yours, but I'm sure she wouldn't want you to fall behind in class." This made Stacy feel like laughing, though she held in all but a small snort. Mrs. Kaufman knew well what Mary Ellis's opinions on school were. Stacy couldn't count the number of times Mary Ellis had gotten in trouble for disregarding lessons, disobeying instructions, or otherwise distracting the class.

"I don't think she would have cared."

Mrs. Kaufman sighed.

"Well, I don't think your parents would like it then."

Stacy frowned. "I understand," she said, though her voice held no emotion.

"Then you can go out to recess with everyone else. Just please try to pay attention or I'm going to call your mother and father."

Stacy nodded and sped from the classroom, her sneakers squeaking on the glossy tiles in the hallway.

As she pushed the blue door open that led to the playground, she was met with the sound of other students who all seemed to be competing to see who could be the loudest. Dust swirled in the air, Stacy couldn't tell whether it was caused by the wind or the crowd of boys who were playing a vicious game of soccer on the playground's small field. Stacy skirted the edge of the field and went past the playground, settling on a bench at the playground's edge. Silently, she stared into the woods that surrounded the back of the school, letting the near summer heat run through her. As she watched, a squirrel scampered out from inside the woods and crossed the playground, running towards the street.

Chapter Four

Mary Ellis had awaited the man checking tickets with confidence. She stood in the long line with her chest puffed out and what she felt was a brave smile on her face. As she approached the tiny podium, watching the man spread out other passenger's tickets and check all of their information. When she passed through his line, he only glanced briefly at her ticket, shoving it back into her hand only a moment after she placed it in front of him.

Now though, standing on the platform, ticket clutched in her hand, she began to feel slightly dizzy with doubt. Men and women towered over her, dragging large rolling bags or briefcases purposefully back and forth. Mary Ellis was on guard, afraid she'd have to leap out of the way of those who passed her. She wished she could sit down on one of the benches that lined the station, but she had never ridden the train before and was worried that if she sat down and relaxed she wouldn't be able to get onto the train before it started. As she waited, Mary Ellis watched the clock. The clock struck one and then passed by it going on to 1:05 then 1:10. Mary Ellis became jittery, what if the train didn't arrive at all.

She glanced around the platform for someone experiencing a similar panic, but most just seemed irritated, if anything.

Eventually, the train pulled to a halt by the platform, fifteen minutes later then it had said it was going to be arriving, and people began to swarm around her, rushing into the car. Mary Ellis followed behind them, one hand placed on her backpack, the other coiled around the plastic bag, keeping it close to her chest. Gran had always warned her about the dangerous thieves that roamed crowded public spaces like sidewalks or train stations.

As Mary Ellis shuffled onto the train car, she searched for a seat. The car was one of the strangest places that Mary Ellis had ever seen. There were rows and rows of blue and red plastic chairs; nothing like the green vinyl of the seats on the bus or the cracked vinyl of Gran's old car that always smelled like some dog had pissed all over the back seat. To be fair, it didn't smell much better here. There was trash fluttering across the floor of the train car as the doors opened and shut. Mary Ellis followed the aisle to the back of the car and took a seat, wedging herself in by the window. She watched as the train car began to fill up, people quickly settling in the train's seats. Just before the train pulled out of the platform, a man rushed on and sat next to Mary Ellis, placing his legs out in the aisle so he had his back to her.

For the first hour and a half or so, everything was calm. Mary Ellis read from one of her books and listened to the conversations of the couple sitting in front of her. The man thumbed through a folder of documents he had sitting on his lap, occasionally pausing to read through one of them or rearrange the order of the documents in the folder. As the couple in front of Mary Ellis were discussing their possible move to DC, Mary Ellis was leaning farther and farther forward, trying to hear them, her book now tucked into her backpack. While she did this, the man who sat next to her began to turn to face forward and slammed into her, dropping his folder.

"Jesus Christ," he said, the papers fluttering to the ground and spreading underneath the seats and around the train.

"I'm sorry," Mary Ellis said, dropping to her hands and knees and beginning to gather papers. The man glared at her and began to do the same. It only took a few minutes before the papers were collected and the man stood up, holding them in one hand and the folder in his other.

"Where are your parents?" He sat back down next to Mary Ellis, who retreated as far as she could into the corner of the seat, clutching her backpack to her chest.

"They-they... my grandmother is sick and my mom wanted me to go see her before she died because she lives in North Carolina and we live in Pennsylvania and I didn't get to see her all that often."

"How old are you?"

"Eleven," Mary Ellis said, seemingly much louder than was intended. As she did, the woman from the couple in front of them spun around and glared at her. The man seated next to her placed his hand on her arm and she turned away from Mary Ellis.

"You're eleven?" the man said. Mary Ellis nodded.

"And your mother let you travel down the whole of the East Coast?"

"My mom says I'm very self-sufficient." Mary Ellis could feel herself shrinking under the weight of the man's scrutiny. She knew what her fate was if he determined that she was not fit to travel alone.

"But why wouldn't she just come with you? It's her mom, right?"

Mary Ellis screwed up her face and tried to look bigger in her chair. "Why does it matter to you?"

"Because if your mother is just going to let you run around causing trouble and knocking shit over I have some things to say to her."

"Well she's not here. Sir."

The man sighed and shoved the folder into his briefcase with such force that Mary Ellis saw it ruffle slightly.

"Is someone meeting you when you get off on the train?" the man said.

"No, I'm just going to meet a friend of my grandmother's when I get to North Carolina."

The man scowled and turned away from her as the train pulled into the platform and the doors flew open. He stood up and exited the train, speeding past other passengers who were trying to exit so quickly that Mary Ellis lost him in the crowd.

Mary Ellis then exited the train, holding her backpack tightly. The terminal she walked into was much larger than the one back at home, with towering ceilings that made the sounds of trains echo through the station. The station was also much more crowded than at home; here, even the benches were taken up by men in ratty clothing who looked like they were asleep, surrounded by trash bags and backpacks.

Mary Ellis's original plan was just to get another ticket to take the train however far she could get, but as she stood in the center of the train platform, her stomach began to growl. Thinking of the money she had in her pocket, Mary Ellis knew she could still afford to buy some nice food, so she exited the terminal, walking up the stairs and out into the sunlight.

Mary Ellis exited onto a cluster of crisscrossed streets and towering buildings. The sky was cloudy, so much so that Mary Ellis couldn't see a hint of blue above her. The buildings that surrounded her were also primarily grey, and the people that sped down both sides of the street weren't much more colorful.

Mary Ellis walked down the street away from the terminal, trailing behind a group of suited men. As she did, she noticed the man from the train walking down the street near her. She stared at him for just a moment, but he didn't glance back at her. As she walked, Mary Ellis caught sight of a tiny pizza parlor. Considering for only a moment, she crossed the street towards it.

She pushed open the door to a dimly lit, crowded restaurant with what looked like a Subway sandwich bar lining the sides of it. She bought two slices of pizza with no toppings or sides, and no drink, as she knew that she could sip from the water bottle she kept with her. Then, Mary Ellis walked over to a booth and sat down.

She listened to the sound of other diners for a little while, but eventually just sunk into her own head. This was the farthest she'd been from her home since she was five and now, instead of being stuck with Gran, she was completely alone. On the surface, Mary Ellis felt strong: she had bought her own ticket, packed her own bags, gotten onto the train all by herself. There was something underneath this feeling that was beginning to stir. Mary Ellis wouldn't call it fear exactly, but in flashes memories were beginning to surface. Mary Ellis's final memories of her mother and father. She was crying, her head between her knees sitting on the floor of their apartment. Her mother wiping the tears off of her face. "We'll be right back. We'll be right back. You won't have to wait very long." That tired, pleading voice that Mary Ellis could only remember hearing once. Then the woman came and stole her. She was fake nice in the same way that Gran was, always using that sweet little voice and batting her eyelashes and pretending that things were alright when Mary Ellis knew that they weren't alright. Mary Ellis knew what awaited if she was unsuccessful, the woman and her little laugh every time Mary Ellis spoke. And the way the woman called her "Mary" no matter how many times Mary Ellis told her that that wasn't her name.

"Hey, kid, I thought you were going to North Carolina."

Mary Ellis's head snapped up. Above her stood the man from the train, a plate of pizza in one hand.

"I am," Mary Ellis stammered, "but I had to stop and get dinner."

"When's your next train leavin' and where's it heading?"

"Well, I'm going clear down to North Carolina next."

The man eased into the booth across from Mary Ellis, grabbing a salt packet from the basket on the table.

"No other tables," he muttered, almost to himself. He spread the salt across the pizza with a sweeping motion, silent. "You're going straight down to North Carolina from here. Not making any stops?"

"I don't know I'm just following instructions."

"Let me see them then. Your instructions." His voice came like a growl from the back of his throat, so quiet that Mary Ellis needed to lean slightly across the table and strain just to hear him over the sounds of the other patrons in the parlor.

"Why do you care where I'm going?"

"Because I don't want a young girl wandering alone in the city. It's dangerous for you here there are people who want to hurt you or worse."

"Just let me get on my way and mind your own business." Mary Ellis stood up and began to exit the booth, leaving an uneaten slice of pizza on her paper plate. As she walked past the man to leave, he grabbed her arm; she could feel his hand shaking slightly as he held her in his grip.

"I ought to call the police and tell them about the child wandering the city streets on her own, but I want to know what you're doing. Just stop and eat with me."

For a moment, Mary Ellis let her eyes fly wildly around the corners of the restaurant, struggling to make contact with another patron, an employee, anyone, but they all seemed locked into their own little worlds. When she knew no one was going to help her, Mary Ellis took a shaky breath and sank back down into her seat, a lump forming in her throat. She forced down a few bites of her pizza, knowing she would need the strength it gave her later in her journey.

"My name is Charles," the man said, picking at his pizza.

"Mary. Ellis."

"Cute name."

"Thanks." Mary Ellis struggled to keep her voice steady, keeping her eyes locked on the ceiling, counting the yellow stains it was marked with. She wished he'd never told him anything. She wished she'd run out of the restaurant while she still had the chance.

For a while, Charles stayed silent, but Mary Ellis could feel his eyes on her and wanted to shift to avoid them. Instead, she stayed focused on the ceiling, taking steady breaths, hoping to steel herself to run, if that was necessary. But the dinner was finished in relative silence, Charles eating only absentmindedly, his eyes never straying from Mary Ellis.

"Are you in danger? Did someone do something to you?" he said eventually, in a hushed tone. This time he was leaned far over the table.

"No. I'm fine."

"Are you running away from your parents? Did they do something bad to you?"

"No." Mary Ellis didn't meet his eyes, instead took in the other patrons of the restaurant: a woman with golden hair who was hunched in front of a laptop, the waiter squeezing his hands on the edge of the counter so tightly that his knuckles turned white, the man he was talking to, a tall stern man with a cartoonish mustache and a frown set deeply into his face.

"Just try to give me a reason why I shouldn't turn you over to the cops? Please. It would really be a hassle."

"I just can't. Leave me alone." A young couple in the booth in front of them, each leaning onto their palms and smiling warmly at each other. A twenty something who had just rushed in, ordered quickly, slipped into a seat next to the wall and was now sitting with his hear craned back, leaning against the wall.

"You're a kid. That would be irresponsible of me and you know that."

Mary Ellis frowned. Charles let out a deep sigh.

"Where are you staying tonight?"

"I don't... know." The manager emerged from a doorway behind the counter, a stout woman with wiry, dyed red hair that she kept in a large clasp. Mary Ellis glanced around the room for a moment, there was no one else, no one to protect her, to shield her from Charles's words. For the first time since he arrived, Mary Ellis turned her focus back to Charles.

"At least let me put you up for the night, there's probably a room available at the motel where I am staying." Mary Ellis was silent.

"Think of everything dangerous that could be out on the streets. Let me help you." Mary Ellis frowned, a motel room could be nice but Mary Ellis felt her stomach churning at the thought that she'd have to go anywhere with him.

"How much for a room?" Mary Ellis asked, slumping farther down into her seat.

"I'd pay for you."

"I don't want to owe you money."

"It's $45, but they wouldn't let you get a room by yourself. You're too little."

"I'll go back with you and you can buy the room for me."

"You have $45?"

"Uh huh," Mary Ellis said. Despite herself, she felt vaguely insulted.

"Well, you must not have a lot, so why not let me pay."

"I have enough."

"Alright, it's your call, but I'd think that's a waste of money if I were you." Charles chuckled, and Mary Ellis stood up. They exited the restaurant together, stepping out onto a dim street.

Mary Ellis stood for a moment, watching the cars pass by as she waited for Charles to turn down the street. Charles followed behind her stopping next to her when she stopped.

"I think I'll just go find somewhere to stay on my own," Mary Ellis said quietly, eyes flicking to the ground.

Charles gently took her shoulder, turning Mary Ellis towards him.

"I think you should come with me. I can't in good conscious let you stay out on the street, especially when I don't know yet if I'm going to turn you over to social services."

"I'd rather just-"

"Or do you want me to call the police now." Mary Ellis was staring up at Charles's face, which had hardened significantly.

"I don't want anything to happen."

"Of course. I just want you to be safe." Charles relaxed his grip on Mary Ellis's shoulder only slightly and began to walk along the street. "We're going to catch a taxi."

Mary Ellis's stomach was twisting into knots.

"Let go of me," Mary Ellis said, stepping out of his grip. Charles sighed.

"Just follow closely," he said, voice tense with anxiety, flagging down a taxi. As it pulled up to the side of the road where Charles and Mary Ellis stood, Mary Ellis glanced back at the pizza parlor, contemplating whether she should run back inside, but Charles was watching her intently.

"It's time to get in."

Mary Ellis turned back to him and he nudged her forward, pressing his hand into the small of her back. Mary Ellis climbed into the back seat of the taxi, watching Charles climb into the passenger's side. He began chatting to the driver, giving him an address to a motel that Mary Ellis didn't even catch the name of. Mary Ellis sat tense in her seat, pressing her hands into its cracking leather.

DC flickered past Mary Ellis as the car traveled towards the hotel. There was so much more action in the city than Mary Ellis had ever seen before, but her heart was pounding too loudly in her head for her to pay attention to the city that swarmed around her. The taxi ride didn't seem that long, but when the car pulled to a stop the clock claimed that twenty-five minutes had passed.

"Come on, kid." Charles smiled, opening the door to the back seat of the taxi. Mary Ellis clambered out, saying nothing. She stood on the side of the road while Charles paid the driver.

"Let's go inside now," he said, shaking her out of a daze that had seemed to overtake her, clogging her ears and causing the world to swim. Charles took her hand and dragged her towards the motel. Mary Ellis barely felt in control of herself, distant from the things going on around her.

Charles marched them up to the front desk.

"Hi, I'd like two singles." Mary Ellis could feel her heart pounding in her ears, he was going to send her back. The woman on the other side of the desk just nodded, clicking a few keys on the computer behind the desk.

"Do you want adjoining rooms?" the woman asked, glancing up from the computer.

"Oh, that would be great," Charles said, leaning onto the desk, shielding Mary Ellis from the view of the woman.

"Alright, here's your room keys."

"Thank you so much." Together they went back into the night air, walking along the side of the building until they reached their rooms.

"I'll give you the money just give me my key."

"Tomorrow we need to talk about what's happening with you. We can get breakfast together tomorrow."

"Give me my key." Mary Ellis attempted to shove the money into Charles's hand, but he refused to take it, placing the key on top of the small stack of money then turning away. Charles then began to unlock his door.

"Listen, kid. I really just want to make sure you don't get hurt."

"How could I get hurt in my hotel room. Alone."

Charles considered her.

"Meet me for breakfast tomorrow. Please." Charles exhaled and pushed his door open without another glance at Mary Ellis.

Mary Ellis frowned, holding tightly to the strap on her backpack. Once Charles had shut his door and she heard the lock turn, Mary Ellis unlocked the door to her room and went inside. The room was a single, with one double bed dressed in drab, ugly colors. On the other side of the room was a window that opened onto a balcony. Mary Ellis had never been on a balcony before.

She crossed the room to the side of the bed closest to the window and put her backpack down. Then, she locked the adjoining door between the rooms. Sitting down on the bed's edge, she stared at the small TV in front of the bed. She scrambled for the remote and turned it on. The TV was turned to a true crime show discussing the murder of a young girl by her mother. Mary Ellis flicked through the channels, looking for something she remembered from home. Something she liked. But there wasn't a single kid's channel she could find. Instead, when nothing piqued her interest, she turned back to the crime channel and leaned back onto the bed, pushing her backpack onto the floor. She pulled the blanket around her shoulders. Burying her face into the pillow, she tried to focus on the sound of the TV.

"Her body was discovered on the side of the road in the trash bag by a man walking his dog," the man on the TV said, little emotion in his voice, Mary Ellis sighed, her mind drawing her to Gran, the cold mass in the bed. Mary Ellis still couldn't tell how she felt about it. Her mind considered sadness for a short while, but that wasn't it. It was something less. Not indifference, she was certainly scared by the things she saw, but that's what it was, fear, not sadness. Fear that Gran's death had been a result of her prayers. Perhaps when the police came they would- No, they could never know it was her. She left no traces.

"The crime was almost perfect, there were no traces of DNA left behind or material from the attacker's clothes, but there was one thing she forgot. Diana was the only one who had seen Patricia that afternoon and claimed to be there for the attack." Hearing this, Mary Ellis felt her body seize. She had been the only one there as well. The police would know that she was the one who had done it. The one who had killed

Gran. Even if they couldn't prove it, the police would know it was her. They would come after her and put her in jail or just give her back to social services who would pass her around like she was a toy. Mary Ellis squeezed her eyes shut.

"We hope that through the evidence we show you on this program you will help us open Patricia's case back up." Mary Ellis switched the channel and some boring talk show filled the room with sound. Mary Ellis snuggled into the bed and listened until she fell into a fitful sleep.

Chapter Five

Sunlight streamed through Stacy's window, waking her from a deep sleep. All night she had tossed and turned, dreaming of times when she and Mary Ellis had been together: sneaking into Mr. Willis's backyard to retrieve the new doll that Stacy had gotten for her birthday, standing far out in the ocean and just screaming while her parents stood on shore watching them, late nights during sleepovers, Mary Ellis laughing at Stacy's fear of the dark, ensuring that Stacy didn't feel too scared. During all of these moments, when Stacy most needed Mary Ellis's presence, she would be there, ensuring Stacy wasn't alone and cowering. Though to be fair, Stacy never would have been in those situations in the first place were it not for Mary Ellis existing in her life.

Sighing, Stacy climbed out of bed, swiping the sleep from her eyes and plodded downstairs in her pajamas. Entering the living room, Stacy could already smell the sweet aroma of pancakes. She guessed her father would be the one cooking them.

Entering the kitchen, her suspicions were confirmed. The kitchen was a disaster area and Stacy's father stood in the middle of it, trying to balance cleaning the counter and flipping pancakes at the same time.

"Here, Dad, let me help you," Stacy said, approaching her father and taking the sponge from him. Her father laughed.

"Well good morning to you, too. You don't think your dear old dad can handle this on his own?"

"I know he can't," Stacy said, starting work on the counters.

"How you feeling this morning?" her father asked, after a moment of silent work.

"I'm just glad to not be in school right now. I'm glad I get to sleep in." Her father put a spatula down and peered at Stacy.

"I'm being serious. How do you feel?"

Stacy turned away. "I'm fine, Dad."

Stacy's father flipped the last of the pancakes onto a plate and turned towards her, setting his spatula down. For a moment he just watched as Stacy swept a pile of flour into her hand and carried it to the trashcan. As she returned to the table to resume cleaning, he placed his hand on her shoulder.

"Listen, I wanted to talk to you before your mom woke up, because she's really pissed about this, but your teacher called us yesterday afternoon. Apparently, she's worried about you not paying attention in class. That you just stare of into space." Stacy stared at her feet, trying to focus on her father's words.

"You don't understand."

"I know you are worried about Mary Ellis right now, but no matter what happens your life is going to go on. If you let yourself get left behind, you will miss opportunities. You won't get to live your life to its fullest extent. You get that, right?"

"I- I-" Stacy couldn't feel anything, her head swimming with an almost floating feeling. The words swelled in her throat, getting stuck. *I know where she is going. I don't know if she can make it without getting hurt or losing me. I don't want to lose her.* "It's almost summer."

"That's not an excuse for you missing out on your life." Stacy's father leaned down so he was eye level with Stacy.

"I'm trying," Stacy stammered, feeling heat boil behind her eyes. The image of Mary Ellis standing in the center of the Minimart, next to the dairy containers was burned into her mind. Much of her time in school was spent trying to shake those images away. To stop her mind from running through the multitude of scenarios that drove Mary Ellis away. To stop her mind from imagining all of the places she could have been, the things that could have happened to her. But even if she managed to distract herself for an instant, her mind would just race back to Mary Ellis. To the photo they put of her on the television when she was confirmed missing.

Her father just sighed.

"I know, honey, I know you're trying, but you just need to push through it."

"Dad, I told you I'm fine. I'm just working on it." Tears slid down Stacy's face. Stacy tried to swipe them away.

"I don't know if you can work alone though." Once again Stacy's father attempted to meet her eyes, but Stacy tried to focus on the corner of the room.

"Please, just let me fix it."

"You can try, but if you don't start feeling better soon I think you should go see someone."

Stacy's father slipped two pancakes onto a plate and handed it to Stacy. She walked to the kitchen table and sat down, watching her father as he pulled syrup out of the fridge and poured it into a cup. He then placed it into the microwave and set it for ten seconds. When ten seconds had passed, he took the syrup out of the microwave and placed it in front of Stacy.

"I'm going to go bring these up to your mom," he said, starting towards the doorway to the room. Stacy nodded, but her father had already left the room. In his absence the silence of the room enveloped her. Once again she could feel the thoughts of Mary Ellis creeping up on her. It settled like clouds in her head, swirling together into almost incoherence. Images of Mary Ellis from their last few days together, the things they had said to each other, the sound of the news casters voice on the TV clustered in Stacy's mind. She pressed her eyes shut, sighing, and leaned over the table. Attempting to shake away the thoughts, Stacy took a bite of her pancakes. Even the taste of her father's special recipe melting in her mouth didn't rid her of the sinking feelings in her chest and brain.

As she sat at the table, eating as best she could, Stacy began to hear her parents voices upstairs, muddied by the distance. Though she couldn't hear exactly what they were saying, Stacy was sure it was about her. She strained to hear their voices, wanting to creep up the stairs and sit outside of their bedroom door as they spoke, pressing her face to their wall so she could hear them. Mary Ellis used to do this wherever they went, whenever she could, relishing in the stories of even strangers, who they'd invent stories about. Stacy couldn't do that now though, unsure that she'd be able to make it back to the table if her father wanted to come back downstairs.

Still, not being able to hear her parents was agony. Stacy wanted to press her hands over her ears to stop herself from hearing the muffled voices. She knew eventually the sound would fade into the background and she could resume whatever she could gather together of her morning, but right now her parents' voices felt piercing to her.

"You should talk to her then."

Stacy heard shuffling in the bedroom, suddenly sure that her mother would be coming down the stairs. Stacy stood up. She couldn't handle another layer of stress to her already burdened mind, and a tense conversation with her mother would do just that. Scribbling a quick note on the pad that was set on the kitchen counter, Stacy left the house for the first time that morning.

She stepped out into the cul-de-sac and was immediately struck by the thick heat of summer. Feeling rejuvenated, she began to walk, first taking slow laps around the circle of grass in the center of the street, then off into the forest behind one of her neighbor's houses. She figured that she knew the woods well enough to guide herself back home. As she walked, Stacy allowed her thoughts to blur, pushing away her parents and Mary Ellis. For the first time in a long time, Stacy's head felt empty. She focused on her footsteps, on observing the things around her. There was a doe, her fawn trailing behind her through the trees, a patch of mushrooms nestled into the crook of a tree, and more crushed up aluminum cans than Stacy could count.

Eventually she broke through the trees then stopped. For a moment, Stacy couldn't figure out why, she was only following instinct and there was no reason for her journey to end here, she wasn't even tired yet. Then she looked up. Before her stood the Minimart.

Stacy took a shaky breath. Something was willing her inside, but she didn't want to go. The doors blew open and a woman walked through them, her young child following at her heels. They brushed past Stacy as she stood. She watched them as they walked through the parking lot and clambered into their car, the young mother strapping her child into a car seat. The car drove a little too quickly out of the parking lot and Stacy jumped at the rush of the two people who hadn't seemed to be in much of a hurry, turning back to the doors.

She steadied herself to go into the store or to walk on, but suddenly she was overtaken by the image of her and her mother exiting the store in a similar fashion, her mother throwing aloof words over her shoulder back at Stacy.

How is that friend of yours, Mary Ellis?

Stacy could see the way they crossed the parking lot. How Stacy climbed into the car and stared over her shoulder back into the store, trying to catch a glimpse of her.

She's fine, Mom.

The way their car kicked up dust as it pulled out of the gravel parking lot, obscuring her view of the store. Then they were gone. Then she was gone. Mary Ellis.

Stacy took a few steps towards the door, gritting her teeth. The wide windows on the door loomed above her for a moment, then flew open, revealing its innards to her. The store seemed so small from this view, only a few aisles lining one side of the building and the cashier's counter on the other side. The dairy containers jeered from the other end of the store and Stacy tried to let her eyes glide over them as she stood outside the store.

"Are you coming in or out? Don't just stand there, you're letting all the bugs in," the man behind the register called to her. Stacy him as the store's manager. Stacy took a few steps into the store and stopped.

"What are you doing, girl? What do you need?"

Stacy barely moved except to turn towards the man.

"I'm sorry," she said quietly, stepping out of the way of the door. The man just sighed.

Stacy felt in her pockets for some money, figuring that she needed to buy something in order to stay. She touched her two front pockets and came up with nothing. Then her front breast pocket and produced a few dollars that her father had given her days earlier. She flattened it out against her thigh and held it up counting one, two, three dollars. Enough for ice cream.

Stacy marched her way to the ice cream freezer, newly focused. When her eyes tried to dart their way to reminders, the dairy containers filled with their gleaming gallons of milk, the doorway and its jingling bell, the man behind the register glaring down at her. Stacy reached the ice cream freezer and pulled the door open. She stared down at the packages below. Selecting a chocolate cone, she released the door of the freezer, which slammed shut with a bang. She turned towards the cash register and strode quickly towards the cashier, staring at the floor.

As she did, the bell over the door jingled once again.

"Stacy?" a voice asked, and for a moment Stacy's heart leapt. She whirled around, taking a deep breath, but when the owner of the voice wasn't Mary Ellis.

"I'll just get this please." Stacy said quickly to the cashier and placed the money and cone on the counter, beginning to shift her focus to the girl who had just addressed her.

"Alright," he said, irritation in his voice, but he picked up the money and placed it in the register anyways. Then he handed her a few cents in change. Stacy stuck the money in her pocket and began to step away.

"You need to take your ice cream," the man said.

Stacy heard the crinkling of plastic and then felt the cone being shoved into her hand. She took it, turning her full attention to the girl, who was watching her expectantly.

"Hello," Stacy said timidly, giving the girl a tiny wave. She recognized her vaguely from Ms. Cane's class, whose lunchtime and recess occasionally overlapped with those of Mrs. Kaufman's class, but couldn't recall her name.

"Sorry, I just recognized you from school. I'm Leah." She stuck her hand out for Stacy to shake, Stacy took it. "I'm in Miss Cane's class."

Stacy nodded. "I remember. Sorry."

The girl was tall with a thick ponytail of dark hair that stuck out from the back of her head. She was beaming, seemingly filled with energy.

"You got ice cream? I was coming to pick up bread for my family, but that's a good idea. Could I sit with you while you eat it? If you're eating here of course. If you aren't you can just go home, sorry." The words seemed to pour out of her mouth, spilling into the air around them. When she stopped, it felt to Stacy as if she had cut herself off, having to hold her mouth closed to avoid talking.

Stacy stood in the silence for a moment, hoping that what she should do would just leap out at her, but nothing did. Stacy had never met this girl before, but it might be nice to be with someone new for a little while. Still, she wasn't sure why Leah would want to be with her unless she was weird and didn't have any friends. Stacy guessed that she didn't have any friends anymore either; maybe she could stand to hang out with someone else, even if they were a little weird.

"No, we should eat together," Stacy said, smiling slightly.

"You wait here let me go get my stuff."

So Stacy stood in the center of the Minimart, watching as Leah flew around the store, picking up a loaf of bread and a strawberry cheesecake cone. Stacy used to get one every single time she came to the store with her mother, but eventually grew out of what she now thought of as the sickly sweetness of the cream cheese flavored ice cream. Leah rushed to the counter when she was finished, quickly paying for her ice cream, and then returned to Stacy's side, still smiling.

"Do you want to go outside to eat?" Leah asked.

Stacy nodded, just as Leah grabbed her hand, nearly dragging her into the parking lot out front. Leah sank down onto the edge of the curb, patting the space next to her. Stacy sank down, peeling the plastic wrapping off of the chocolate cone, which had already begun to melt because of the time she had spent in the store, and started to eat. She stared out into the heat of the parking lot once again, sparse with cars.

For a moment, she watched people drive past on the main road, but the parking lot, at least in this moment, was stagnant. Stacy sighed. She felt locked in place too, unsure of how to talk to someone she didn't know well. The last friend she had truly made was Mary Ellis, but they had met two months before kindergarten began and that seemed so long ago. The air in the lot hovered around her and she tipped her head back, looking at the sky. Far above her and airplane was flying. It seemed to move sluggishly through the sky but at least it was moving. Soon it flew out of her vison.

"Stacy?" Leah said, jolting her back to reality, "Are you okay?"

"Sorry, um… yeah. I just was zoned out."

"No, I totally understand. With everything that's happened to you you must have a lot to think about." Leah clasped her hand around Stacy's wrist.

Stacy locked eyes with her for a moment, before turning to stare at the pavement. Her heart had begun to speed in her chest, she wasn't sure if Leah would really be referring to Mary Ellis, if everyone truly knew how lonely Stacy was without her.

"What?" was all Stacy could manage.

Instantly, a blush darkened Leah's cheeks. "I'm so sorry. My mom always tells me I need to think before I speak, but I never do. I didn't realize that, that you..." But her statement trailed off into nothing, and they lapsed into silence once again.

"It's okay, you don't have to worry about it. I was just," Stacy paused, considering what would make her sound the least boring, "surprised. No one's really talked to me about it except for my parents."

Stacy's gaze returned to her cone.

"Really?" Leah asked, for once remaining silent. Stacy watched as a trickle of ice cream slipped down Leah's hand, falling onto the pavement below them.

Stacy nodded.

"If you ever want to talk about anything, I'd be happy to."

Stacy blushed; they'd only just met and already she felt comfortable around Leah, but she wasn't sure what there was to say about life with Mary Ellis that wouldn't sound pathetic.

"Thanks," Stacy said, finishing off the last of her ice cream and turning her full attention to Leah. She watched as Leah polished off her treat as well, wrapping up the stick that once held her ice cream in its plastic packaging.

The heat felt as if it was threating to melt Stacy herself, so when she was sure that Leah was finished, Stacy stood up.

"I should be heading back now," she said, staring down at Leah, "I didn't really tell my parents that I was going out.

Leah grinned. "Are you sure? Mom wouldn't care if you came over to hang out. If you want to, of course." Now Leah stood, next to her, Stacy could see how tall she truly was, towering over Stacy by a few inches.

"Maybe some other time."

"Alright, I'll see you around then," Leah said, picking up the plastic bag of bread that was lying next to her on the sidewalk.

"See you," Stacy said somewhat reluctantly. Leah had already begun to walk across the parking lot and disappeared quickly out of view, leaving Stacy alone.

Figuring there was nowhere else for her to go, Stacy thought it was time to head home. She walked out of the parking lot and back into the woods, nervously retracing her twisting steps from earlier that morning.

Faster than she would have liked, Stacy arrived back at her doorstop. She stood at the end of her paved walk for what felt like a long while, but eventually moved to the door. Then she opened it.

"Stacy?" Her father's voice echoed from inside the house, it seemed to be filled with a mixture of anger and worry.

Stacy smiled slightly, relishing in the delight of breaking rules, and stepped into the kitchen, where she believed she had heard her father.

"I'm here, Dad," she said, watching him sweep into the room to see her. He pulled her into a hug, but when it broke, he was frowning.

"Don't leave without telling me," he said sternly, keeping a hold on her wrist. She jerked it out of his grasp.

"I left a note." Stacy pulled away from her father. "You don't need to worry about me."

"You can't just leave whenever you want."

"I'm fine." Stacy frowned, she was nearly in middle school, she should be able to walk to get some ice cream on her own.

"Don't forget you're only twelve," he said, but Stacy could tell his anger had already faded.

"I'm going to go upstairs and get something done, okay?" Stacy asked.

Her father nodded and she walked past him and up the stairs, heading towards her room. She passed the bathroom door and was about to breeze past her parent's room, when she stopped. The bedroom was empty, her mother must have left earlier that morning. Stacy moved past the door, towards her room.

Chapter Six

Mary Ellis awoke bleary-eyed, sprawled across the mattress. For a moment, her heart leapt, suddenly confused at where she was. She sat up, slowly coming to terms with the unfamiliar room. Mary Ellis eased herself off the bed. Standing, she began to feel the effects of the last few days on her body. She stripped off her clothes and walked to the shower. Turning the handle to start the hot water, a small trickle of tepid water streamed out. Sighing, Mary Ellis stepped out of the shower.

Walking back to the bedroom, Mary Ellis pulled a fresh outfit out of her bag and stuffed her old clothes back into it. She turned off the television, sinking down onto the bed. In the moment, all Mary Ellis wanted to do was stay in bed and sleep some more, but the threats made to her the night before and the worry that the police were now coming pulled her out of the exhaustion, so she forced herself to stand up and pick up her bag. She eased herself towards the doorway, taking one last look around the room. How nice it would be to stay here, to spend her days sleeping and watching television, but already Mary Ellis was starting to feel restless. She was going to run out of money soon.

Exiting her room, Mary Ellis started down the hallway towards the stairwell, feeling uneasy in the empty halls. All of a sudden she heard a door slam and spun around, seeing a small man hobbling out of a doorway with a cane. Mary Ellis felt her shoulders relax and continued down the hall and into the stairwell. As the door to the stairwell swung shut, once again she was plunged into silence, finally taking a moment to stop and enjoy the morning.

Mary Ellis walked slowly down the stairs, listening to her footsteps echo off the high walls. All of a sudden, she thought that the footsteps seemed to double, the sound of echoes increasing. Then she heard it.

"Mary Ellis?" a voice behind her asked, she didn't hear the door open or close a second time. Turning around, Mary Ellis faced Charles, standing in what looked to be his pajamas.

"I'm leaving."

"We need to talk about where you're going. You could get hurt, killed."

"Why don't you just worry about yourself?" Mary Ellis paused, considering, "Or your own kids."

Charles just sighed, starting down the steps towards Mary Ellis. Mary Ellis whirled around and sped down the stairs towards the door, hearing footsteps thundering behind her.

"I don't want to hurt-"

Mary Ellis heard a door slam far above her and Charles went silent. Mary Ellis felt a flood of relief rush through her. She wasn't alone anymore. Mary Ellis pushed closer to the door, ready to burst out into the lobby, but she almost froze when she felt a hand grab onto the back of her backpack. She jerked forward, trying to make it to the end of the stairwell and to the door, when she felt something split. All of a sudden the weight on Mary Ellis's back felt lighter and she burst out through the door into the lobby. Stopping short as she saw people milling about Mary Ellis stood frozen in the lobby. Slowly, she walked to the small seating area and sat down. Pulling off her backpack, Mary Ellis surveyed the damage, her backpack hung open on her side and some of her clothes were missing from the inside. She patted around until she was able to find the money towards the bottom of the pack and when she did, Mary Ellis sighed and leaned back into the chair. The backpack had completely split down the side, making it totally useless to travel with. She shoved as much as she could into her plastic bag, letting what wouldn't fit hang in the husk of the backpack at her side.

She hefted herself out of the chair, gathering her salvaged items in her arms. Mary Ellis watched as Charles entered the lobby, smoothing out the front of his shirt. She worried for a moment about her missing clothes, but Charles was starting towards her and she wasn't willing to risk seeing him again. It was time to go, so Mary Ellis, things in hand, slipped down a long hallway that led out of the building through a back door. She flung open the door, unsure of whether Charles would be following her, and rushed outside.

As Mary Ellis sprinted down the street, winding her way through crowds of people, she half looked for somewhere to get a new container for her things. She saw a Target a little down the road and headed inside, the crisp air of the store surrounded her. Wandering into the backpack isle, Mary Ellis gazed at all the different options available. She would need something bigger now, to fit the shell of a backpack and anything else she might acquire on her journey. Picking up a large backpack, she glanced at the price tag. Thirty dollars. Mary Ellis had that, but it was almost a third of her money. She couldn't part with that much money, so she placed the backpack back on the hook. Mary Ellis would need to use only plastic bags. Mary Ellis headed to the grocery aisles, where she picked up a box of Pop-tarts for breakfast. She then sped to the cash register, eager to get on her way for the day.

Mary Ellis watched as the man in the front of the line argued with the cashier about something. In that moment, the tension balled within her and she felt like she needed to flee, Charles could be close. She wanted to get as far as she could away from the city. From Charles. Instead, she tried to focus on what was right in front of her.

The woman standing in front of Mary Ellis in the line scoffed and stared down at her cart, rolling her eyes at the man. The manager seemed to be coming over and guiding the man away. After a few minutes, the cashier gestured for Mary Ellis to come forward and pay for her items. Quickly, Mary Ellis placed her items onto the conveyor belt and shuffled forward, digging around in her pocket for her money. She paid the cashier, who rang her up without speaking to her. Mary Ellis picked up her things and rushed out the door without saying thank you.

As Mary Ellis stepped out onto the street, she began stuffing her things into her bag, keeping her Pop-tarts clutched in her hand. She leaned on the wall outside, letting her backpack hang over her shoulder, and tore open the box of Pop-tarts. She took out one silvery package and tore that open as well, beginning to stuff the contents of the package into her mouth. For a moment the prickle of anxiety that had settled on her shoulders after that morning's meeting with Charles returned, and Mary Ellis dropped her backpack, hung her bags around her shoulders again and started off down the street.

Mary Ellis knew she'd spent too much money. Once, to think she could have spent that much would have astounded Mary Ellis, she had never made a journey like this, but always assumed it would be cheap. Just two or three bus rides and she would be in North Carolina. Now, Mary Ellis didn't know if she could make it.

Mary Ellis could only consider getting away from Charles. She wasn't sure exactly where she was going at the moment, but knew that if she wanted to go anywhere, she would probably need to catch another train.

Mary Ellis wasn't sure where she was in the first place. The city crisscrossed around her in a way she had never experienced before: the buildings looming above, almost seeming to curl over her, threatening to close in. For a while, she wandered somewhat aimlessly through the streets, hoping some indication of a train station would jump out at her, but after a while it just seemed futile.

Somehow, Mary Ellis ended up on the edge of a park with a large fountain in the center. An unfamiliar sight to Mary Ellis, who was used to her parks being accompanied with swing sets and slides, unkempt. Mary Ellis swept herself through the arch that led into the park, heading for a bench facing the fountain, where she could take a moment to regroup. As she did, a woman with a stroller was breezing across the square. Mary Ellis who was starting to jog, feeling the rush of nature in her, slammed into the woman, nearly toppling her stroller over.

"Jesus," the woman yelled, taking a moment to right her stroller.

"Sorry. I'm so sorry." Mary Ellis could feel her head buzzing.

The woman sighed. "It's fine." The woman looked down on Mary Ellis in pity. "Are you alright, honey?"

"Yeah, I'm okay," Mary Ellis said, starting to move away, but then she stopped and added, "Do you know where the train station is from here?"

The woman patiently gave directions to Mary Ellis who thanked her profusely and when the woman's baby started to cry, Mary Ellis scampered away.

Mary Ellis tried to follow her instructions as quickly as possible; it was midmorning and Mary Ellis wanted to make sure she had as much time as possible to get moving. She tried to push all thoughts from her head as she walked, afraid that she would be overwhelmed by thoughts of those she was leaving behind and those who might catch up to her if she lingered in the city for too long.

She approached the station as the sun was high in the sky. Mary Ellis darted quietly through the front door and was once again swarmed with people trying to catch the train. Approaching the ticket booth, she stood on her tip-toes to speak to the ticket salesman, a large man who looked to be in his mid-twenties.

"Are there any trains going to Pineville, North Carolina today?" Mary Ellis asked quietly, fishing around in her pocket for money.

"To Pineville?" the man asked. Mary Ellis nodded.

"No trains go to Pineville from here, but I can show you the connections that you could take to get there." Mary Ellis nodded once again and the man pulled out a map from behind the counter. With a pudgy finger, he traced a route that required three train connections to reach even the edge of North Carolina. With a Sharpie marker he circled each one of the trains she'd need to take.

"You got that?" he asked, holding the map out to her.

"Yep," Mary Ellis said, and then considering," how much would that be all together?" The man paused, glancing up at the ceiling, Mary Ellis could almost see him counting in his head.

"$54, if my math is correct." Oh. Mary Ellis's heart sank. It was too much. After a moment of consideration, Mary

Ellis realized that she would only have thirteen dollars left if she took this journey. Mary Ellis wouldn't even end up in the city where her mother lived and didn't know how long she would need to travel in order to get there. The map wavered in her hands.

"When does the next train leave?" she asked quietly, resigned.

"At 4:45 this evening."

Mary Ellis slipped back into the crowd without another word. She couldn't afford the journey, which would leave her lacking money for food and shelter. It would leave her with no room for error. She would need to sleep on the street that night and try to find some other way forward. Never had Mary Ellis been on a journey of this enormity before. She wasn't sure how long it would take or what exactly she would need, but she was almost sure of one thing: no more hotels and no more spending. For the first time in her life, Mary Ellis didn't have a bed, anyone could take her things or even take her, but she couldn't risk the monetary danger that the bus would force on her.

Mary Ellis walked out of the station and into the newly darkened street. She decided to head for the park, knowing that it was at least south of her, something about it, though small, energized her, and she would need that energy for the days ahead.

Chapter Seven

Darkness hung like a blanket over the park. The streetlamps had flickered on and hummed with electricity. Bugs buzzed around the lamps, adding to the collective hum. Mary Ellis had arrived there late in the afternoon, by this point hungry and slightly exhausted. She sunk down on one of the benches that surrounded the park and hunkered down, scrunching up her jacket beneath her head. She shoved the plastic bags behind her back, it was slightly uncomfortable because of their bulk but Mary Ellis figured that it was the best way to keep her things safe. Bunching into the tightest ball she could manage, Mary Ellis squeezed her eyes shut. As she lay there, Mary Ellis could hear the rush of cars and people around the nearly deserted park. The light and the sounds kept her up, burning into her head. She took a shirt from a bag and pressed it around her ears, but it only sent the light into a dim fog. Mary Ellis didn't know where to find darkness, so she pressed her eyes shut until she fell asleep.

The next morning Mary Ellis awoke to the wide eyes of a woman who was staring down at her. She blinked, her bright face opening at the sight of Mary Ellis's awakening.

"Honey?" the woman said. It was the same woman as the day before, pushing her baby in a carriage. Though Mary Ellis was familiar with the word, it sounded strange in the woman's mouth.

"I'm leaving," Mary Ellis said quickly, already picking up her backpack.

"No, no, are you alright?" The woman reached for Mary Ellis's arm.

"I'm fine." Mary Ellis's mouth was thick with the cotton of sleep. She didn't have her toothbrush. She forced herself off of the bench, barely thinking. Grabbing her backpack, she scampered away.

"Are you okay?"

Mary Ellis could hear the woman calling after her, but she was already trying to block out the sound of the older woman's voice, rounding the corner of the concrete wall that surrounded the park and nearly rushing out into traffic.

Mary Ellis felt like a rat. A vermin. Like she had no place in the world. Departing from the park, she forced herself to head South. How much she would love to get the train right to North Carolina, so her parents could take her in and she would no longer have to run. She could finally feel embraced by her family in her home. Still, the idea that she could be left in Pineville with almost no money haunted her. If anything happened she wouldn't have a cushion to fall back on. What else could she do but press on?

Before she left, Mary Ellis wanted to check if the bus was an option. It could be a cheaper, but the more time she spent in the city, unmoving, the more money she would have to spend and the longer it would take her to get to her family.

Mary Ellis pushed down the street with her backpack in tow, her legs heaving underneath her, still creaking with mid-morning exhaustion. Quickly, she came across a small convenience store.

She slipped inside behind a couple of tall men Mary Ellis could barely tell apart. It didn't matter, she pressed past them and into the open spaces of the store. The lights hummed above her and she scanned the aisles for a moment looking for where she could purchase a map. She paced quickly though the store's small aisles but came up with nothing. Mary Ellis would have to keep looking. In the meantime, though, she'd utilize what she had.

Mary Ellis went to the counter at the front of the store, where a small teenage girl was leaning against the counter, looking bored. As Mary Ellis approached her, she took in her face. Her eyes were so thick with mascara that her lashes looked like spider's legs and the lipstick that covered her small mouth went just slightly too far outside of the line of her lips. On her breast was a nametag that said "Hello! My name is" printed on it and "Cheryl" written in a loopy scrawl.

"Hi, how may I help you today?" Cheryl's voice was unnaturally bright as she stared down at Mary Ellis, suddenly extending her body to its full height from its slouch.

"I'm just looking for directions." Cheryl smiled, her deep red lips stretching, but not parting. Her eyes just looked tired.

"Where to?" She placed a hand on the counter, her nails were curved into little pink almonds.

"The bus station."

Cheryl gaze turned towards the counter.

"I don't know the way," she said breezily. On one hand her fingers tapped on the edge of the counter, her other hand gripped the edge of the counter. "Are you lookin' to purchase anything?"

"I'm fine."

Cheryl's brows furrowed.

"Well, honey, why don't you step out of line then.There are other people waiting behind you."

Mary Ellis slunk away from the counter, watching as Cheryl sunk back behind the counter into a more relaxed state. As she walked out of the store, Mary Ellis watched as Cheryl began to ring up the customer behind her.

As Mary Ellis started down the street again, she cursed at herself. All she could think of were those times that Gran would demand and get exactly what she wanted. Even a month before now, Mary Ellis could recall a trip to the shoe store when Gran had nearly screamed at the cashier who wouldn't give her a cash refund on a pair of sneakers she had bought for Mary Ellis.

"I didn't pay to get shit," she'd spat, a dribble of spit clinging to her chin. Mary Ellis had just leaned against the counter and waited for the argument to be over, as she so often did. She didn't want to tell that the hole had been punctured in the bottom of her sneaker because she had been burning some old schoolwork and had to rush to stamp the fire out. She didn't want Gran or the cashier to know who the true cause of the conflict was.

After twenty minutes the man had given Gran a full cash refund for the shoes and Gran was whisking Mary Ellis out of the store, swearing that they'd never shop at the Payless ever again.

If Gran had been with Mary Ellis now, she would have demanded the girl take them seriously. She would have told the girl to go into the back and look up where the bus station was for them. That she printed the directions out and highlighted the way there. Gran had a strength which Mary Ellis didn't have, couldn't have: to be taken seriously. Mary Ellis wished she could convey the same fury as her gran could, swelling up, turning her face beet red, but even if she did that she would still feel so much smaller than anyone else. Even those her age were often bigger than she.

Mary Ellis continued down the sidewalk, searching for somewhere she could ask for directions. Eventually, she reached a small deli and wedged her way in. The store was heavily crowded with people eating or rushing around. Mary Ellis stood in line behind a group of others, waiting to talk to the cashier, who was a large hairy man who gestured wildly as he spoke to the other patrons. She figured she probably wouldn't get anywhere with him either, especially if a teenage girl wouldn't listen to her, but she needed to get farther before the day was over. Slowly, the line snaked up until Mary Ellis was standing next to the register. The man peered at her.

"What're you getting, kid?"

"Oh, nothing, I was just wanting to get directions to the nearest bus station."

"Here, I'll give you the number and you can call on the phone over there and get directions." He swept a hand over his sweaty brow and pointed a fat finger at the phone hanging on the wall behind the counter. Then, with only a few keystrokes on the computer he sat in front of him, the man leaned down low across the counter and scribbled a number on a sheet of paper, passing it to Mary Ellis.

"Have a good day kid."

Mary Ellis just nodded, walking behind the counter and over to the phone. She placed a call to the bus service, asking about the prices for a trip to North Carolina and which buses she would need to take. After hanging up the phone she leaned against the wall for a moment. It would only leave her with $27. Not much more than if she had taken the train. Mary Ellis figured she could walk some of the way there. She had always been one for playing outside and relished the long walks she would sometimes take to avoid seeing her grandmother, so she assumed she could go far in one day, and when she got tired she could take the bus short periods. She would have to eat less. The food she had purchased would sustain her for a short while: she'd have to conserve her resources, making sure that she rationed out everything that she had. Mary Ellis would need to be more conscious about what she purchased from now on.

With her map in hand, Mary Ellis set out from the station, winding her way through the DC streets with a newfound confidence that the map gave her. Close to the edge of the city, Mary Ellis found the buildings thinning out as the moon crept over the horizon. The cars passing by her began to come more slowly and the heat gave way to a crisp evening cool. Mary Ellis started to feel drowsy, but pushed on, hoping that she would be able to make some headway before the next day.

The moon crept higher, and Mary Ellis found herself just barely inching across the map. Sleep pulled at her and, with the growing urge to sink down into the ditch along the side of the road and lay down, Mary Ellis found herself straying from the path trying to find somewhere where she could spend the night.

She wandered through increasingly dense forest until she could only faintly hear the sound of cars rushing down the highway that would let her find her way back to it the next morning. She pressed herself into the ground placing a shirt under her head and nestling herself into a small bank of dirt.

Though during the day she had felt comfortably warm, sometimes even a little hot and sweaty, now the slight chill that blew through the air filled Mary Ellis with discomfort. She considered taking some of the clothes out of her bag to wrap around herself, but was worried about them fluttering away as she slept.

After some time, Mary Ellis couldn't tell how long, she considered standing up and walking some more. Sleep wasn't coming to her. That wasn't exactly true though, exhaustion weighed on her bones keeping her locked to the ground, only able to hear the cars off in the distance. Every creak in the woods and stick that broke made Mary Ellis leap out of her skin, increasing the length of time she spent lying on the ground.

Mary Ellis keep her eyes closed, trying to block out the noise, but eventually something else crept into her thoughts.

You need to get yourself together kid. It was Gran. Gran was dead.

Mary Ellis sat up, dusting the leaves off her shoulders. She glanced around, once again ensuring that no one was around, then answered.

"I'm trying." She pulled her knees up to her chin and stared off into the distance. The wind rustled through the trees.

You know what I would do if I were you? I would pull myself up and keep moving or I would go to sleep, none of this loafing around feeling sorry for yourself business that you're carrying on with.

Mary Ellis pressed her chin into her knees, her hands clutching at the wet earth beneath her. She was trying.

"Maybe if you'd let me..." Mary Ellis started, but her words just trailed into silence. It wasn't fair to blame Gran, at least not for this, who would have expected this to be the place where Mary Ellis's life would lead. Mary Ellis's stomach swirled with guilt. Even now, apart from her, Mary Ellis couldn't stop arguing with Gran. She didn't even feel that bad about her dying, even if she had been the one praying for it.

Mary Ellis waited for what felt like hours in the dark, but Gran's voice had left her, so she eventually lapsed into sleep.

The sun had barely risen over the horizon when Mary Ellis was shaken from her sleep. She sat up quickly, hearing the leaves crush under her almost dramatically.

Breathing heavily, she leaned forward into her hands. Her mouth felt thick with morning breath. Feeling it was as good a time as any, she reached into her bag and fished out her box of Pop-tarts. Tearing open one package she scarfed down one of the Pop-tarts and began onto the next one in the foil packet, but after taking one bite she stopped. She needed to save her food for later on the road and she'd had enough now, though she wished that she could eat until she truly felt full. She slipped the box back into her bag, slipped the bags over her wrists and then started towards the road.

"Good morning highway," Mary Ellis said. "Good morning cars." She stared upwards. The bloated clouds drifted through the sky, unaware. Mary Ellis walked on, the silence over coming her.

The cars seemed to be rushing down the highway at faster speeds than they had been the previous day, sending a thrill through Mary Ellis as she trudged down the highway. Mary Ellis at first tried to look at her map of the whole coast, but it wasn't detailed enough, so she shifted to her map of only DC vowing that she'd get a map of Virginia the next moment she had. It was terrifying how long the coast seemed to be, even if she wasn't going all the way down it. She had to make it though; she had to be with her parents once again. Maybe she'd need to take the bus some more. Maybe she'd need to spend every last dollar, but it would be worth it. It had to be. Mary Ellis had no other choice.

Either way she would figure it out. She'd have to. Then when Mary Ellis met up with her parents she would have all sorts of stories to tell them about her travels.

***

"Daddy! Daddy!" Mary Ellis screamed, her tiny feet pounding the floor. As her father opened the door, Mary Ellis flung her way into her father's arms, a large t-shirt draped over her head that hung down nearly to her knees. "Come see what Mama's doing."

She'd take his broad hand in his and drag him into the kitchen. When her father had peeled off his jacket he pulled Mary Ellis into his arms. He'd fling her above his head and spin her around. He'd tuck her under his elbow and carry her into the kitchen. He'd place her on his shoulders and let her play with his hair. Mary Ellis would babble and babble to him and her mother. She'd help them cook dinner and they would all eat together, clustered around the table. Like a family. Finally.

***

Not that Mary Ellis remembered any of that. She'd just read it in the postcards. Mary Ellis pulled one out of her bag; it was one of the oldest ones. Her favorite. On the front was an image of a coastal street, but that wasn't the most important part. In the note on the other side of the letter, her mother had said that they'd just eaten lunch on that street and that the restaurant they'd went to reminded her of Mary Ellis. Then she'd shared that memory of her, running to greet her father whenever he arrived home.

Mary Ellis wished she had a memory of it. She wished that she knew all of these little things that her mother seemed to know. Now though, she only had a few tiny memories from when she was only five and the letters.

Mary Ellis walked through the day and into the night, not stopping when the sun went down. Though she was tired, Mary Ellis needed to get as far as she could each day for this to really make a difference in her journey. She would take the bus when she could, but walking needed to be important if she wanted to save money on her trip.

It was only when she reached a rest stop that Mary Ellis decided to stop for the night. She trudged up the pathway to the small building that held the bathrooms and a small guest area with a stack of pamphlets on the corner. There were a few cars and a large truck parked in the parking lot, but it seemed like every person that they once held had gone missing.

Mary Ellis walked down the dimly lit sidewalk towards the bathroom. She tugged on the door to the women's room, hoping to wash her face in the sink and use the restroom rather than peeing in the bushes in the woods next to the rest stop, but the door didn't budge. Instead, Mary Ellis walked over to the picnic tables that sat in the grass next to the parking lot and slipped the backpack off her shoulder. She unzipped the bag and pulled out the peanut butter and bread, making a quick peanut butter sandwich. She slouched at the table, her bags surrounding her, paying no mind to the world around as she ate.

As she lay hunched over the table, she scratched at its wooden surface. 'ME' she wrote in tiny letters, then underneath it 'Stacy.' She stared at the letters for a moment. Maybe Stacy would be able to talk. Mary Ellis retrieved Gran's phone and flipped it open. The screen didn't turn on as it always did when Mary Ellis had used it before. She'd only used it a couple of times, so she wasn't sure there wasn't a button to turn it on. After searching for a couple of minutes, Mary Ellis couldn't find it. The battery must be dead.

Sighing, Mary Ellis took a new T-shirt out of her backpack and slipped it on overtop of the shirt she was already wearing. Then she pulled her arms out of the sleeves of the shirt she was wearing underneath and shimmied out of the shirt, glancing around to ensure that there was no one watching. Mary Ellis pulled a pair of pajama shorts from her bag and carefully changed. A woman who was crossing back to her car caught Mary Ellis's eye, looking disgusted. Mary Ellis just gave her a small smile, hoisted her bags over her shoulder, and turned, walking back just past where the woods met the clearing carved out by the rest stop.

In the closest to pajamas she could get under the given circumstances and trying to disappear into the trees, Mary Ellis lay down on her side, using her backpack as a pillow. She watched the street light closest to her flicker slightly, until she was too tired to keep her eyes open and fell into sleep.

Chapter Eight

Stacy should have been happy right now. It was the first day of summer and the sun was blazing through her window. Already, she could hear the sound of children playing down in the street. Almost every day through the summer huge groups of kids would run around the cul-de-sac playing soccer and screaming. Even early in the morning the kids would tear through the circle of grass. In the past, the sounds lightened Stacy's spirit, Mary Ellis always came over on the first day of summer, but now it just reminded her of the long lonely days ahead. The house was empty aside from her. Her father had already gone to work and her mother was just out. During the week, Stacy's mother went out with her friends: they had brunch and went to exercise classes together.

Stacy got out of bed and walked downstairs, cooking a quick breakfast of eggs, slightly burnt but Stacy was just learning. She could handle it. Stacy had summer work to do, the middle school reading list seemed to be a mile long and her math teacher had given each student a big packet of problems that they had to complete before school started, ensuring they were ready for the complexities of sixth grade mathematics, but now this was only the first day of summer and Stacy didn't think she should start so early, not while all the other kids were playing right outside her door.

Instead, she took a shower then dressed, trying to avoid the obvious thoughts about what she would be doing right now had her best friend not abandoned her. When she was finished, Stacy walked outside, unsure of what she wanted to do. She walked on the edge of the street as far as she could from the children playing, who didn't even turn to acknowledge her as she passed. As she approached the edge of the street, Stacy began to see cars speeding down the road that crossed with hers, this street was a popular cut through and her father always chided her when she wanted to walk it because it had no sidewalks. He seemed to think that she would walk through the middle of the road, right into oncoming traffic. He seemed to think that she was so young that she didn't know that she could just walk across people lawns. He didn't want her to leave, he wanted to keep her trapped inside the house, her home, a baby swaddled in between the walls. Stacy knew she would be okay as long as she was home before her parents arrived, though she wasn't sure exactly when that would be. It would be some time, though they didn't like to leave unless they would be gone for a long time.

Stacy had never really been able to explore her town. Other than the Minimart, which she wasn't interested in returning to, her mother went into the city in order to shop for furniture or new clothes, usually alone, but Stacy was sure that she could find something to do in this town. Stacy wound her way through streets of uniform houses. She saw many other kids as she walked, those whose parents let them be free.

Eventually, she broke through the barrier of houses and entered onto a street that was lined with small shops. She passed by a small boutique filled with flowery white clothes,

Stacy couldn't see a single color inside. She also passed by a bookstore, which she might resort to later in the year, when she had to get her summer reading books or had run out of everything to do. There was a movie theater at the end of the street that Stacy had heard her mother talking about pretty frequently. She went with her best friend to see the latest rom-coms, and then occasionally told Stacy about them when she arrived home late at night to see Stacy on the sofa watching her own movies. Stacy had visited once with her parents on her birthday, but she was so young she barely remembered it.

When Stacy reached the end of the street, the only thing that was left was the highway. She had wound her way through the streets of her town and now it was behind her. Stacy peered out at the speeding cars. She wanted to cross the road, to see what was beyond her town, but she could already feel fear squeezing her heart. She wanted to feel in her heart what she knew was true, that what her parents wanted for her didn't matter. That she was her own person who couldn't be constrained by them. She wanted to move past this town and head out into the world. To leave all of the people who had never helped her with anything. Who had never spent their afternoons playing in Stacy's backyard or doing baking experiments in her kitchen. Who never walked through the woods pretending to be fighting monsters and collecting garbage to be made into gifts for fake creatures or each other. Who left her alone while Mary Ellis kept her safe and sane in this stupid tiny place. Suddenly she felt a wave of sadness. Mary Ellis was gone. She had crossed this highway without fear and continued on to her future. Even if she called when she reached her parents, Mary Ellis would still be living in North Carolina while Stacy was stuck here. Stacy hadn't thought like this before. She had simply wanted her best friend to succeed and followed her almost blindly. She had thought that she was protecting Mary Ellis, but maybe Stacy should have told the police. Mary Ellis would have been sent back to the town, maybe Stacy's parents would have let Mary Ellis stay with them. She could have slept next to Stacy on the floor and it would be like a sleepover every single night. Stacy couldn't do that now. The police would kill her if they realized that she hadn't told them everything she knew.

Or, Stacy wished that she could have taken Mary Ellis up on her offer. She didn't know how that would have worked, Mary Ellis was so much stronger than she and the search for them would have surely been more ferocious had Stacy's parents been looking for her. She loved her parents, too. No matter what, she still loved her mother and father and didn't want to leave them, no matter how much she pretended otherwise.

Stacy sighed. She was still alone. She looked out to the buildings across the road, a department store and McDonald's. Behind the stores a wooded hill rolled, dotted with small houses and stores stretching as far as the eye could see. The world seemed so wide here, as though if she looked closely Stacy could see Mary Ellis trudging towards North Carolina. Stacy knew it wasn't possible. There was nothing she could do about it. Stacy was alone and in a way, Mary Ellis was, too, but Mary Ellis was finding her way to a new family, people to cure her loneliness.

Her shoulders slumped. She turned from the highway and began to walk back towards the town. Sometime soon she would find a way to show her parents the way she felt. She would find a way to make them see her. For now though, she would have to wait. Stacy would just go home. Walking home, Stacy crossed paths with the kids on the street, this time not bothering to shy away from them. She just blazed on through and walked up to her door. It seemed to loom above her, Stacy's heart throbbing in her throat. She pushed the door open.

"Where have you been?" Her mother's voice rang out across the living room. Stacy's heart seemed to fall ten stories to her feet.

"I was taking a walk."

Her mother sighed, she was draped across the sofa, watching a remodeling show on the television. Stacy crossed through the room, trying to make it to the kitchen before more questions rained down on her. As she reached the doorway, her mother turned towards her, sitting up.

"You need to tell us where you are going."

Stacy stopped, turning towards her mother.

"Mom I'm-"

"We're already worried about you and when you just leave we get nervous. You're not an adult. You can't just do whatever you want."

Stacy sighed and turned back towards the kitchen, taking a few more steps into it.

"I don't need to be babied."

"Something happened to you, Stacy, life's just not going to be the same despite it."

Stacy started up the stairs, wanting to shrink under her mother's gaze. Her mother narrowed her eyes. She sighed.

"Stacy, talk to us."

"I just need my space." Stacy continued, trying hard not to turn around.

"We're your parents."

Stacy rolled her eyes, but felt her breath hitch as she passed through the kitchen to the fridge. Swinging the door open, Stacy grabbed a yogurt and a spoon and passed back through the living room, casting a glance over at her mother who was already leaned back, staring at the television once again.

Stacy marched upstairs and headed to her bedroom once again. She peeled the top off of the yogurt and set it down on her bedside table, wanting to ensure that she finished everything she needed to do before she ate. She ran to her desk and threw open the drawer, rifling through the papers and school supplies she had shoved inside. She knew she had some money stashed away. She wanted to waste it this summer. When she couldn't find it, Stacy turned to the closet and opened the door. Pushing aside piles of clothes, a small shoe box was revealed to her. Stacy sank down onto the floor and pulled the box onto her lap, knowing she had found what she was looking for. She shimmied the taught rubber band off of the box and pulled it open. Inside was all the money she had been saving since she was in second grade. She pulled $25 out and tucked it into the top of her shirt. Tomorrow she was going to go to the movies. She would get lunch and get out of the house.

Chapter Nine

Mary Ellis awoke to the sweeping of flashlight beams in the clearing next to the rest stop. The woman. She must have called the police and now they were after her. Mary Ellis's head was reeling as she pulled herself into a sitting position and then onto her feet. Sticks and leaves crunched underneath her body, sounding as loud as thunder as the police approached the edge of the forest. Mary Ellis grabbed her backpack in her fist and ran away from the lights. She heard a feminine voice mutter to a male one, but Mary Ellis was tearing through the forest, the blood pounding in her ears. She heard something, presumably the people, moving in the brush towards the edge of the clearing. She tried to press faster through the brush, which tore at her arms and threatened to pull her towards the ground. They were going to get her. They were going to take her back to Gran's house and she would never meet her parents and this couldn't be the end. This couldn't be the end of her journey.

Feeling her lungs burn, Mary Ellis pushed herself as far as she could then collapsed onto the ground, her chest heaving. She kept silent for a moment, listening for the heavy footsteps of police running through the brush. Hearing nothing, she gagged, rolled onto her side and heaved. The hum of the forest around her and the pain in her chest made Mary Ellis want to stop right where she was and fall asleep, but she knew the sticks she was lying on would hurt her back in the morning.

Mary Ellis stood up and stumbled through the brush, looking for somewhere she could collapse for the night. In the moment, her body felt ragged, her clothes hung off her body, dirty and torn from the branches, her breath heaved in her chest, making her double over in fear and exhaustion. Blood leaked from her face and arms, stinging only slightly, but she didn't feel enough pain to stop it. She paused, listening deeply for the sound of footsteps rustling in the forest once again. There was silence for a moment, then rustling quiet and too far off to be a concern. Finding a dense mat of leaves at the base of one tree, Mary Ellis collapsed onto the ground, gathering herself in a tight ball and stuffing her backpack under her head. She fell quickly into a deep sleep.

Though sleep came easily that night, Mary Ellis was not allowed peace. In her dreams Gran came, her body warped and rotted. Mary Ellis hadn't seen it since the morning when everything changed, but here in her mind the damage that had occurred since then was crystal clear. Mary Ellis approached the body, her heart thundering in her chest. She grabbed the corpse's arm and turned it over, so Mary Ellis could see Gran one last time. But the face the body had wasn't its own. It was Mary Ellis's. Then, it was her mother's.

Mary Ellis jolted awake to the sound of rustling right beside her and sat up, her breathing heavy. For a moment she was paralyzed, the fear of being in Gran's house, of seeing her mother, overtaking her. Then the sound receded into the forest, seemingly just an animal that had come upon her, the strange girl in the forest alone. Mary Ellis let out a breath she had seemed to be holding and looked up; the sun was high in the sky. It must have been almost midday. She let out a string of swears.

Then the pain came. Cuts dotted her face, arms, and legs, encrusted with dried blood and exertion had made her limbs aches. She howled in anger, then sealed her lips. Mary Ellis was completely unsure about where she was in relation to the highway and the rest stop. The police could still be chasing her. They could be anywhere in the woods. Mary Ellis could only half care. She was exhausted. She wanted to curl back up and sleep some more, but she needed to keep moving.

She needed to find her way out of the woods and figure her way back to civilization. First, though, Mary Ellis needed to eat.

Taking out the last silver package from the Pop-tarts box, Mary Ellis scarfed down the first Pop-tart from the torn open package. Still, her stomach ached. She knew she should save that last Pop-tart for dinner that night. That she would survive perfectly fine without eating it. But she was hungry. So she stuffed it down and threw the empty box and wrapper onto the forest floor.

Mary Ellis stood up and glanced around her, looking for something that could help her get back into the city, but she couldn't see anything that would tell her where she came from. There were trampled branches and sticks everywhere and she wasn't paying enough attention the night before to recognize anything that could be used as a landmark. If she started to walk, Mary Ellis would end up somewhere, so that's what she would do. She slung her backpack over her shoulders and just picked the direction she felt would point her back towards the road.

The walking was unlike any exertion Mary Ellis had ever experience before. She had thought gym class was bad, but this had to be one hundred times worse. The sun dragged over her, beating down on her head and shoulders until they were burnt crisp. She had guzzled down her water, hoping it could keep the sun from her, but all it allowed were momentary glimpses at cool. Then the water was gone.

By the time the sun was touching the horizon and night was beginning to fall over the forest, Mary Ellis had seen nothing. Once, she thought she spied a wooden platform in a tree far above her head, but she couldn't make out any indication of life within it.

She stopped only for a quick dinner as the sun went down, smearing together half of a peanut butter sandwich. She watched as the sun blazed towards the horizon, peeking from behind the trees in oranges and pinks and reds.

***

"Sunsets are best when you've worked hard all day," Gran said.

Mary Ellis peered up at her for a moment, resisting the urge to sneer. If Gran had a moment to put Mary Ellis down, she would never let it pass. Mary Ellis was tearing the husk from ears of corn, shoving them into a plastic grocery bag that was sitting on their rusted patio table. Gran took a drag from her cigarette.

"Yes, they're more beautiful when you truly work hard and don't spend all day slacking off with your friends, embarrassing your grandmother."

Two hours ago the school had called; Mary Ellis was failing her math class and would have to repeat third grade again. Gran should get her a tutor or bring Mary Ellis in for extra instruction from a teacher.

At first it was fire, Gran screaming and telling Mary Ellis that she better get her grades up that she better pass the third grade or else she wouldn't be able to go outside for the entire summer. Mary Ellis was screaming about how she didn't care, how she didn't want to go to school anymore. But after a little while, everything went calm. Not peaceful but calm. Stagnant. The air was full of tension, but Mary Ellis had nowhere to go.

She sulked around her bedroom, avoiding her homework, until Gran told her to come down and make the corn for dinner.

Now, Gran was waving her cigarette at the horizon, a plume of smoke seeming to trail from her palm.

"Say something," she said suddenly, jabbing her cigarette at Mary Ellis. Finished with husking, Mary Ellis took the corn over to the grill.

"I'll try to work harder," she said quietly. All of the ears of corn didn't fit side by side on Gran's tiny grill, so Mary Ellis began to stack them one on top of the other. She struggled to light the grill, waiting for Gran to continue.

"Do you have anything else to say?"

"I'm sorry," Mary Ellis whispered as the grill leapt to life.

Gran grunted, heaving herself up from the patio chair. She dropped her cigarette butt onto the porch and crushed it with her foot. Mary Ellis heard the patio's screen door creak open, keeping her eyes locked on the grill.

"Remember to flip those in a couple of minutes." The screen door slapped shut.

***

Mary Ellis polished off the sandwich and stood up, her mouth dry from the peanut butter. Mary Ellis wished she would have saved some water. Now though, the sun was just a few minutes away from slipping totally beneath the horizon, but Mary Ellis knew it was time to continue on.

So she kept going. She kept walking when she saw a fox slipping between a slight gap in the trees, sneering at her. She kept walking while the wind began to whistle in such a way that it almost sounded like human howling. She couldn't stop.

When night fell, the forest began to weigh down on Mary Ellis like a thick blanket pressing on her eyes, willing her to sleep, but she pushed on. Past small valleys and caves that looked like the perfect place to stay that muggy night, where she could have dreams outside of the horror that she seemed to be consumed with at the moment.

When she began to think her legs would give out beneath her, just as the sun was beginning to rise, Mary Ellis saw it. The light between the dense trees had begun to grow brighter. The trees were thinning out, the forest must be giving way to something else. Anything else.

With a renewed burst of energy, Mary Ellis made her way through the trees towards the light that she saw. Everything seemed to grow brighter as she went, the denseness of the forest giving way. She wanted to scream with joy. Mary Ellis broke through the trees and walked out onto a highway. She couldn't be sure that it was the same highway that she had peeled off of the night before, but it was somewhere.

Mary Ellis felt exhausted, nearly delirious and parched. Though the sun was rising in the sky at this point she needed to lay down somewhere, let some time pass so that she didn't collapse on the side of the road. Ensuring that she kept the road in her sights, Mary Ellis crept off into the bushes at the side of the road and laid down. The moment her head hit the ground, she fell into a deep sleep.

***

By the time that she woke up, the moon was already in the sky. Mary Ellis stood up dusting off her clothes and picking up her bags. Her stomach ached in hunger once again, but Mary Ellis wanted to get somewhere recognizable before she spent any more time standing still. She wanted to be sure she could get her bearings, that she was even going in the right direction. Now she just needed to continue.

Mary Ellis made her way back to the road, choosing the direction that she most believed would lead her down the coast. She couldn't be sure though, being all turned around from her run through the forest.

The night passed with little event, each time that a car passed Mary Ellis she would shrink back towards the forest, afraid that the people were after her still. Eventually, though, she even acclimated to the sounds of people rushing by her, and continued down the road with more ease. The sun rose and began to make its way through the sky, but there was little in the way of buildings. Mary Ellis's feet had begun to ache like the rest of her body and the blood from her cuts and scrapes had dried on her body, leaving rust colored stains all over her skin and clothing.

Midmorning, exhausted, Mary Ellis passed a massive 'Welcome to Virginia!' sign, and finally knew that she was heading in the right direction. In that moment, sure of where she was, Mary Ellis sunk to the ground and, leaning against the sign, made herself a peanut butter sandwich. She ate with her head leaned back against the sign post, watching as the cars sped by her. When she was finished, she tucked the loaf of bread back into her bags and started back down the road.

After a couple more hours of walking, Mary Ellis passed by another sign, this time advertising many things that you could stop by around the area. It advertised for a large rest stop only a little ways ahead. When Mary Ellis saw a turn off that lead up to a large concrete building, she took it. There were only a few cars in the parking lot, but as Mary Ellis made her way closer to the building, she could see the names of the stores above the building's door. There were a variety of fast food restaurants and a Starbucks as well as a gas station. Tucked behind the largest building was a CVS. At the sight of the CVS, Mary Ellis got a burst of energy. She wanted to run, to reach the stale conditioned air and buy something to eat.

To go to the bathroom and wash herself off. To go into a stall and get changed. She couldn't run though, her whole body hurt.

As Mary Ellis reached the automatic door, which flung itself open, she almost cried at the sight of the store. The wide aisles and tinny pop music playing from the ceiling comforted her and she pushed herself through the doorway and headed quickly down an aisle, grinning an almost maniacal grin.

She scanned the shelves, she tried to avoid looking at the food, figuring she had all she needed for a short journey, but she couldn't ignore the gnawing hunger inside her. She grabbed a pre-packaged sandwich from one of the open coolers, a treat for the hardships she'd faced over the past twenty-four hours. Then she walked to the cosmetics aisle and grabbed the cheapest available suntan lotion, washcloth, and the smallest available bottle of hydrogen peroxide. Collecting everything in a basket, Mary Ellis headed to the front counter. The woman who stood there looked disinterested. As Mary Ellis approached, the woman's eyes widened and she sat up, turning away from her large beige computer.

"How may I help you today?" the woman asked with raised eyebrows

Mary Ellis dumped the contents of her basket onto the counter and pulled the money out of her pocket.

"I'm just getting some things for my mom. We're taking a road trip down to North Carolina."

When Mary Ellis stopped speaking the woman peeked out into the parking lot. She frowned, but turned back to Mary Ellis.

"That so?"

Mary Ellis nodded. The woman scanned Mary Ellis's items slowly, leisurely, looking bored.

"Your total is $14." The woman seemed to have distanced herself from her own actions. She looked away from the girl in front of her. Mary Ellis counted money out and placed it on the counter. She had $42 left.

"Thank you for your business."

"Thank you," Mary Ellis said, then remembered, "where is your bathroom?"

"We don't have one."

"Please, can I use the employee bathroom? I know you have one." The woman sighed and nodded. She led Mary Ellis to a door next to the counter, above it read 'Employees Only.' She unlocked it and held it open for Mary Ellis, who slipped under her arm and walked into the center of the bathroom. The door slammed shut behind her and Mary Ellis relaxed, dropping her plastic bag to the floor. She turned around and locked the door. Though her stomach and throat ached, Mary Ellis knew she needed to wash quickly and get out of the store.

First, Mary Ellis plugged her phone into the outlet under the sink. Then, she pulled out the washcloth and hydrogen peroxide. She peeled off the wrapper and opened the bottle, then soaked the edge of the washcloth in the peroxide. Gently, Mary Ellis soaked her cuts in peroxide. When she was finished, her whole body stinging, Mary Ellis wet the washcloth and rubbed her body down and slathered on sunscreen. She tried to get most of the dirt and blood off of her body, but Mary Ellis was exhausted and hungry and wanted to leave. The lights felt harsh to her and the music was grating. Still, Mary Ellis found it in her to change into a different set of clothing. Though the clothes she had left were dirty, there were no cuts and scrapes. She considered discarding the clothes she had just removed, but she didn't want to lose anything she might need in the future.

"What are you doing in there, kid?" The woman began pounding on the door. For a moment, Mary Ellis was frozen. The slamming of the woman's fist against the door sent a shiver down Mary Ellis's spine. An image flashed through her mind of her cowering in her bedroom, fear pulsing through her. Her grandmother was pounding on the door, sending things falling to the floor.

"Nothing. I'll be out in a minute," Mary Ellis stammered and flew to the toilet. Quickly, she used the restroom, filled her water bottle up, grabbed her phone, and scampered out the door.

"Thanks," she mumbled to the cashier.

"You have a good one," the woman said, her voice slightly irritated. Mary Ellis pushed quickly out into the parking lot and scampered around the side of the building. When she reached a point that she felt was suitably off the road, Mary Ellis sank to the ground and pulled the sandwich out of her bag. As she tore into it, Mary Ellis instantly felt her muscles relax. She leaned up against the building and took her time eating. She felt like she was enjoying each bite of the sandwich more than anything she had eaten before in her life. When she finished eating, Mary Ellis crunched up the plastic wrapper and shoved it into her backpack with a sigh, easing back into the wall. Mary Ellis knew she should move on. She knew she should keep walking down the road until the sun set. Then she should sleep, but Mary Ellis was so exhausted. She needed to at least rest.

First, though, Mary Ellis needed the reaffirmation of Stacy, and now that her phone was a little bit charge she could call her. She dialed Stacy's number; it was the only one she knew by heart. The phone rang and rang, eventually going to voice mail.

Mary Ellis sunk down against the wall, shaking. Though a mixture of adrenaline and fear coursed through her, Mary Ellis knew she needed to at least try to rest.

Mary Ellis walked behind the building and into where the grass was high. She sunk onto her side and curled up in a ball, draping a T-shirt across her eyes to block out the sun. Mary Ellis shut her eyes and lay down for as long as she could manage. Still, the sun blazed through her makeshift mask and sleep wasn't coming, so Mary Ellis stood back up, packed her things and started down the road. She could at least make some progress before night fell.

***

As Mary Ellis pushed down the road, the buildings became closer and closer together. Soon the streets were lined with businesses and Mary Ellis felt her heart leap. She began to see people going from place to place. Though they avoided her, Mary Ellis wanted to run over and squeeze them until they burst. She wanted to be held. She wanted to be in her mother's arms or for her father to hoist Mary Ellis over his shoulder and swing her around like he used to when she was small. Mary Ellis could still be small.

Mary Ellis pushed on through the town, looking for somewhere to sleep and waiting for nightfall. She passed by a small restaurant and a flower shop, dotted in between tiny houses with fences around the front yard. There was a bakery. It almost made Mary Ellis swoon, the smell of sweet buns wafting into the street. She had to be strong, though, sugar would give her nothing but comfort. She felt it was the only thing she needed, but deep down she knew that she didn't. Mary Ellis spotted a small park off down a side street. It was next to the elementary school, but Mary Ellis was pretty sure summer had begun by now. As she followed the road, she felt a lightness in her feet. She felt her shoulders ride as she stood taller, an air of ease coming over her mind.

Mary Ellis quickly reached the park and surveyed it, a small smile growing on her face. The plot of land was wedged between the school and yellow house that was the same exact shade as Gran's house. The house that won't be her home for much longer. She would be settled on the sofa between her mother and father in a short time, eating dinner on the couch while watching cartoons. Actually, it didn't matter what they were doing. They would just simply be together and that was all that Mary Ellis needed. That was what she would get.

On a whim, Mary Ellis walked the perimeter of the park. Tracing her hand along the playground furniture. The monkey bars reminded her of Stacy, swelling her heart fondly. Stacy was the worst at monkey bars; she never made it more than two bars out without falling flat on her ass. Mary Ellis smiled. That's why they always strayed past the playground. They played in the field just behind the low metal fence that blocked off the playground from the woods. Mary Ellis and Stacy would pretend to be cats or monsters or warriors. They would make up wild stories about their travels through fantastical lands. In their minds, Mary Ellis and Stacy would speed through time and space away from their school and the town where they always felt bogged down. Together. Together they would do everything. They would go through life together, becoming everything they talked about when hanging out at Stacy's house, lying on her crème colored plush carpet and staring at the ceiling.

Suddenly, Mary Ellis felt tears prick her eyes and squeezed them shut. She tore her eyes away from the monkey bars and headed towards the edge of the fenced in park, where there was a tiny enclosure over a circular slide. Mary Ellis climbed the stairs and crossed over the swinging bridge. Smiling slightly, Mary Ellis remembered when she used to treat these things like play. She would run around these playgrounds on weekends when school was out because that was the only way that they could avoid all the other children. Mary Ellis entered the small blocked in building, looking down the tunnel of the circular slide. She placed her bags down and lay down flat on her back, staring up at the enclosed ceiling of the cabin.

Mary Ellis looked out across the playground; the sun had dipped down over the horizon and the sky blazed with stars. There was a calmness and serenity in this night time. No cars rushing by and though she was objectively in a more dangerous situation than she had been in the past, she was in a place with more people, after all; it was almost like Mary Ellis could feel the weight of them there with her. She felt a comfort with people around her, like she was a part of the world again. Mary Ellis didn't need to fall quickly into sleep, she didn't feel desperate for it, and she just let herself drift into the haze of sleep.

Chapter Ten

Two days later Leah called Stacy nearly buzzing. She wanted to take Stacy to the comic book store the next town over. Leah's favorite comic was releasing a new issue that day, something that was hurriedly explained to Stacy by Leah on the phone. Leah needed to know right at that moment because she was about to get in the car and Leah needed to know whether they were coming to pick her up. Stacy was planning on going to the bookstore that day, but she knew that she was just becoming friends with Leah. That if she abandoned her now then Leah would stop calling, so she'd go.

Stacy had just barely woken up and walked downstairs when the call came. Her father was currently making breakfast, frying up some eggs and bacon and Stacy was barely dressed, hardly ready to go out. But Stacy felt like she should go if she wanted to continue being friends with Leah.

"Dad?" she asked, placing the phone on the table next to where the phone hook was.

Her father turned to face her. "What sweetie?"

"Can I go out with one of my friend's now?"

Stacy watched as her father cast his eyes down at the pan. She knew he must be confused. *What friends*, he would think, *who could she possibly have?* Stacy felt a pang of anger, though she knew his thoughts were justified.

"Who?" he said eventually, not taking his eyes off of the pan.

"Her name is Leah. We just met."

"Can I meet her mother?"

"Dad, she said I needed to be quick."

Stacy's father rolled his eyes. "Fine."

Stacy picked up the phone. "I can go," she almost yelled, "but I've got to go get ready now if I'm going to be ready in time."

"Okay," Leah said, her voice bright, "I'll see you in about five minutes. My mom got your address from the school directory. You know for Valentine's Day and stuff? Wait, you didn't move, right?" Leah seemed almost out of breath by the time she was finished speaking.

"No, we didn't move."

"Okay, you have to go. Bye."

"Bye," Stacy said, but Leah had already hung up the phone. Stacy bolted up the stairs and changed as quick as she could into going out clothes. Then she shoved a couple of dollars into her pocket and ran back down the stairs.

She could only yell, "See you later, Dad," as she watched Leah's car pull up in the driveway.

***

At the comic book store, Stacy could barely get a word in. From the moment Leah stepped into the store and waved goodbye to her mom, she was spouting off knowledge about her favorite series and pacing around the store pointing at various things that she knew and giving small greetings to the staff who she recognized.

"This is like, my spot," Leah said in one moment, tucking herself back into a corner that was stocked with obscure indie comics. She pulled a few comics from behind one of the shelves and sank down to the floor, passing one to Stacy.

"I wish I had a spot," Stacy said, easing herself to the ground. Stacy tried to think of what place she could call her own. Her bedroom would be the closest spot, but even that felt less than hers, being decorated by her mother when she was still a baby. She didn't even feel like she had interests, at least not in the way that Leah did. She didn't like comics or any specific book series, and she could never become so comfortable that she could know every employee from a store by name.

"You'll find one eventually," Leah said. "I think that everyone does."

Stacy watched as Leah flicked open one of the comics to reveal a tall, blonde girl wearing armor and surrounded by a wreath of fire. She looked so strong, powerful, surely she had a spot.

"What's wrong?" Leah asked eventually, "Don't you want to read?"

Stacy stared at her hands; she didn't really want to read this. It was a third or fourth issue of something she'd never read before and it looked like fantasy, which Stacy wasn't really into, but she couldn't bare letting down Leah. What if that made her want to leave?

"No, I'm fine. Sorry." Stacy flicked open the comic book and stared at the first page. It was a detailed illustration of a woman relaxed in bed surrounded by trash. She smiled; it reminded her of Mary Ellis.

For the next couple of hours, Stacy and Leah chatted and read comics. When they were finished, they walked around the shops outside: a bookstore, a consignment shop, a vintage toy store. They were all clustered together around a little courtyard, which they finally sat in when they had explored everything else the shops had to offer.

Stacy was getting hungry by this point, having forgone breakfast in order to make it to Leah's on time, but felt odd suggesting that they do anything that Leah might not want to do. She had asked Stacy to come along, after all, so Stacy just hoped that Leah would get hungry as well.

"We should head over to the arcade," Leah said at one point, interrupting her own train of thought. The arcade was the one building in the complex that Stacy and Leah hadn't touched. It hadn't been open at the time they arrived and only now could they see an acne-covered teen in a polo shirt unlocking its door. "I brought quarters."

Once again, Stacy felt a twist in her gut. She hated the arcade, there were too many flashing lights and sounds, and she thought the boys who perched themselves against the machines to make fun of the others or got far too into the games they were playing were terrible to be around. Instead, Stacy was staring at a bowling alley across the highway, a stout, blue building with a massive bowling pin exploding painted on the side of it. Stacy wasn't sure why bowling was calling to her so much in this moment, when the sound and lights would probably be similar to that of the arcade, but she wanted so desperately to ask Leah if they could go. If they could cross the highway to gorge themselves on greasy nachos and jam their feet into ill-fitting bowling shoes.

"Stacy, are you coming?" Leah asked, now standing to the side of the table, staring down at the girl next to her.

Stacy took one last look at the bowling alley, considering telling Leah that that was where she really wanted to go, but decided it wasn't worth the risk. Stacy couldn't lose another friend, not with Mary Ellis gone, so it was better to be unhappy with someone than unhappy with no one at all.

"I'm coming," Stacy said. "Sorry." She stood up from the table and began to follow Leah towards the arcade.

***

Stacy returned home sporting a brand-new tattoo after a few hours in the arcade. It was temporary, of course; Leah had gotten them while Stacy was in the bathroom for a moment of quiet and calm. She hadn't asked what design Stacy had wanted, picking out a bomb for herself and a flame for Stacy, which they then applied with water from the bathroom tap. Stacy stared at the place where it marked the inside of her wrist as she opened her front door. It was already peeling, and barely looked like what it was originally meant to be. Stacy should have pressed Leah to apply them both to herself.

Stacy sighed and stepped through the doorway into her living room. Already, her mother was sprawled out on the sofa, flicking from channel to channel on their television.

"How was your day?" her mother asked.

Stacy was slipping off her shoes and placing them into the bucket that her mother had placed next to the door, to prevent Stacy from tracking mud all over the house.

"It was okay," Stacy said, but her mother didn't respond. Stacy watched for a moment as her mother settled on a talk show and leaned back into her chair. She assumed that their conversation was over and pulled her phone out of her pocket, pressing the button in the center to turn it on. When the screen didn't flick on, Stacy walked to plug her phone into the charger on the side table.

"What did you girls get up to?"

"We-" Stacy started, but at that moment her screen flickered to life and Stacy saw she had one missed call. From Joyce Walker. Mary Ellis.

Stacy needed to be alone. She needed to call Mary Ellis back because she knew that's who it was. Mary Ellis was probably in danger; she probably needed Stacy's help and was going to get hurt because she wasn't there. Now Stacy had to contact her to make sure she was okay.

"had fun," Stacy stammered, already continuing up the stairs.

She did not see her mother turn around, but assumed she was staring back at the television already. Stacy ran up the stairs, letting herself breathe heavily as she crashed onto her bed, already dialing the phone. Mary Ellis didn't answer.

For a moment Stacy stared at the flame peeling on her wrist, suddenly feeling a wave of bitterness. She should have been there. Mary Ellis needed her. Instead, Stacy was out having fun with someone who Mary Ellis had never met. She had abandoned Mary Ellis just had Mary Ellis abandoned her, but it was worse because Stacy had no reason to have done it. She began to scratch at the mark on her wrist watching the red and orange flake away. Tomorrow, Stacy would have to stay home, to wait by the phone, just in case she received another call. If Mary Ellis needed her, then Stacy had to be there for her. Leah could wait, her own wants could wait. Stacy had only Mary Ellis to worry about.

Chapter Eleven

Mary Ellis woke up late the next morning, feeling rested, the sleep had seeped into her bones. She sat up, the warmth of the air around her like a thin blanket. She slathered together another peanut butter sandwich and scarfed it down. Then, Mary Ellis delved into the leisure of the morning. She slid down the slide, landing on the woodchip-covered ground of the playground. Then she started down the street, drinking in the sight of the town.

Though she knew that she should start down the road towards North Carolina, she wanted to linger in the town for a few more hours. Mary Ellis thought she deserved a break anyways; she was exhausted from the past days struggle. Just for a little while. So, Mary Ellis walked back down the street she had come from into the heart of the town. She walked past the tiny shops that lined the street. The whole town seemed to have a sparkling veneer over it, a warm blanket of normalcy. It was so perfect.

Eventually, Mary Ellis was lured into the tiny bakery she had seen the day before. She pushed through the heavy wooden door into a small room that was thick with air the scent of yeast. Two circular wire tables were placed in the window of the bakery, overlooking the street, and three large cases filled the other half of the space open to patrons. They were laden with sweets, everything from loaves of bread to sticky buns to piles and piles of cookies with various colors and flavors of icing. The smell of the sticky buns almost made Mary Ellis swoon. If there was one thing Gran could do, it was cook, and she would always make sticky buns like those when she'd have her friends over. She'd spend the whole morning angrily cooking and cleaning, spitting about how Mary Ellis shouldn't leave the house so disgusting and swatting her hands away from the pile of treats. Mary Ellis would have to sneak one off of the table of desserts after the ladies had come over and Gran was off chatting with them in the living room. Mary Ellis walked up to the counter and ordered one of the heavenly smelling sticky buns. The man behind the counter passed it to her in a crinkly wax paper wrapper. $3. $39 left. Mary Ellis sighed, a knot forming in her stomach, but walked to one of the tiny tables and sat down. She had just had breakfast, but wasn't able to save it now, so she dove in.

As she ate, Mary Ellis watched the town pass by through the window. She saw families walking together, the children bounding in front of their parents, clearly thrilled about where they were going. Even the people who were walking alone seemed to be happy, or at least contented to be going to wherever they were going. Mary Ellis guessed that this was the way it used to be when she lived with her Gran, but now she was watching. Now she could look in at the world without being a part of it. The thought made Mary Ellis smile. The sun beat down on the people of this small town, but still they went about their days content.

All too quickly, the sticky bun was gone. It wasn't as good as the ones that Gran used to make, but it was still delicious. She crushed up the wrapper and threw it away. Then, sighing, she walked out the door.

Back on the street, Mary Ellis walked in and out of stores, gazing in the copious amounts of antiques and refurbished furniture. She walked through the tiny garden in the back of a flower shop and along the bank of the bay which bordered the side of the town. She stared down at the swirling blue black waves. Though the water was murky and almost ominous, Mary Ellis couldn't see anything malicious lurking beneath its depths.

For a long while, Mary Ellis watched a group of other children playing along the edge of the water. They had to be about her age, running and playing alongside of the bank. She could see their colorful swimsuits bobbing on the edge of the waves. There was a rope hanging out over the water and the children were swinging out and crashing into the water, sending a huge spray out onto the others, who all screamed and reeled back. Then they burst out into a cacophony of laughter. Mary Ellis wanted to run to them all. She wanted to peel off her shorts and dive into the water with them. Instead, Mary Ellis just settled for taking off her socks and shoes and wading up to her knees in the water. She stood for a long while, watching them play and cooling off her feet, before she saw one of the children, a tall girl, look up and make eye contact with her.

Mary Ellis watched as the girl splashed across the river towards her, some of the other children trailing behind her, a mother duck and her ducklings. She approached Mary Ellis with a smile on her face. Mary Ellis guessed that she was around her age, with long red hair hanging past her waist so the tips of it just brushed the water. She was in a pink swimsuit dotted with hearts, but it didn't seem to fit with the way she stood. She seemed tall and well, cool. Mary Ellis stared at her own feet and attempted to retreat onto the bank of the river.

"Hey, kid," the girl said. "How old are you?" Mary Ellis looked up and, in doing so, met her eyes.

"I'm eleven," Mary Ellis said, her shoulders slumping. The girl smirked.

"You don't look eleven." Mary Ellis looked down at herself, the oversized shorts and child's T-shirt didn't really help her to look mature. Not knowing what to say, Mary Ellis just stood there, watching the girl. "That's no matter, do you want to come swim with us. It's pretty hot out here."

"I don't have a swimsuit," Mary Ellis paused, then watching another child splash into the water off of the rope swing. "But sure."

"Come on. I'm Jess."

"I'm Mary Ellis." They were splashing along in the murky water. Shells and stones crunched underneath Mary Ellis's feet. When they reached the middle of the river, where the water was deepest, Mary Ellis had to hoist her backpack over her head to avoid getting it soaked. The water was barely above Jess's waist the whole way across.

"I've never seen you here before, Mary Ellis." The current tugged on Mary Ellis's waist, threatening to pull her downstream, but she pushed on.

"I'm just passing through here."

"Alone?" Mary Ellis nodded. They reached the other edge of the bank and Jess turned towards the rest of the children who were playing.

"This is Mary Ellis, she's cool." Mary Ellis smiled shyly and held up her arm in a kind of tiny wave. The kids nodded at Mary Ellis, then kept on playing, turning their attention away from her. Jess waved her onto the bank, and then walked over to a log that was propped up on two rocks, as a sort of bench.

"So where are you heading, Mary Ellis?" Jess sat down and patted the log next to her. Mary Ellis sat next to her.

"I'm going to visit my parents in North Carolina."

"North Carolina, from here?"

"Yeah, it's exhausting." Mary Ellis leaned back to look up at the sky, puffy clouds were floating across it. Flies buzzed through the sour smelling air, landing on tall grasses. There was calmness here.

"Are you walking the whole way there?" Jess was staring at her. Mary Ellis met her eyes, folding her feet into a pretzel so she was sitting cross-legged.

"No, I'm trying to take the bus when I can, but I don't have a lot of money." Mary Ellis didn't know why she trusted Jess. Maybe it was because she was close to Mary Ellis's age, but seemed to be so much more mature than her.

"That sucks."

"Yeah."

For a moment they lapsed into silence, watching the squealing of the other children as they splashed in the water. Maybe Mary Ellis just missed having someone to talk to. Maybe she just needed to feel like she wasn't alone in the world.

"Why do you need to visit your mom?" Jess asked, kicking patterns into the sand.

"I used to live with my grandmother," Mary Ellis said, then she sighed, "but she died and I don't want to go into foster care or some shit." God, Mary Ellis couldn't have sounded more forced. Jess was staring at her feet, which were pushing tracks into the rocky sand of the beach.

"Sorry."

"I guess it's fine. It's not like you could do anything about it."

Jess's face contorted in a strange way; Mary Ellis couldn't recognize her expression.

"Does anyone else know?" She looked up at Mary Ellis. Someone in front of them plunged into the waves.

"I don't know."

Jess just nodded, processing.

"I'll see if I can do anything to help, okay?"

"Alright." There was another pause. "Come on this is getting depressing. I want to have a good time." Feeling the thrill of taking charge, Mary Ellis grabbed Jess's hand and pulled her towards the water. Though her shorts had mostly dried from their trudge through the river, Mary Ellis didn't care. She marched into the water, letting the oily mud that lined the bottom of the river squish between her toes. Rocks occasionally jutted beneath her feet, threatening to slice them to bits, but Mary Ellis didn't care. The other children weren't avoiding her exactly, they just didn't know her, and Mary Ellis was fine to float on her own at first.

For the rest of the afternoon, Mary Ellis felt like a kid again. She guessed she still was a kid, but the weight of her journey had settle on her shoulders and become familiar to her. Now though, she felt free. The group had spent most of the afternoon playing in the river, but eventually, when some of the younger kids had begun to shiver, they climbed out and dried themselves on the bank, slipping into dirty T-shirts and shorts as they did. Then the kids, once again complaining about the almost consuming heat, decided to go to get ice cream. At first, Mary Ellis's heart began to twist, afraid that she was going to have to spend more money. Upon seeing Mary Ellis's look of anxiety though, Jess assured her that the shop they were going to employed one of the other children's brother, who would give them ice cream for free. When they arrived at the shop, they walked around to the back door and were greeted by the brother, who quickly made them all vanilla cones, swearing at his younger sister and chiding her about how much trouble this would get him in with his boss. The other children just laughed this off, so Mary Ellis did too. Even when the sticky vanilla ice cream was running down her hands, Mary Ellis just smiled and tried to eat faster, licking around the edge of the cone to catch the drips. Most of the afternoon's conversation was meaningless, chatter about the beginning of summer and the teachers the rest of the children were leaving behind. Sometimes they laughed and made inside jokes that Mary Ellis didn't understand, but she didn't care. The afternoon felt like a dream, like Mary Ellis had been absorbed into the happiness of the golden town. Every once in a while her mind would flicker to the road ahead, but she couldn't bring herself to leave. Besides, the free food was useful.

It was only when the sun went down that kids started peeling away from the group and going home. Mary Ellis had never had anything like this before, the meaningless collective of kids, just having a good time. All she'd ever had was Stacy.

When they reached a squat brick house, Jess waved Mary Ellis over. Mary Ellis weaved her way through the crowd to Jess's side.

"This is my house, you should come for dinner." Jess started up the cement walkway and Mary Ellis followed her onto the porch.

"Okay, thanks-" Mary Ellis started, but it seemed that Jess was just expecting her to come without a word, because she continued.

"I'm going to ask my dad if he'll drive you some of the way if that's cool. I'll do it after dinner in case he says no, okay?"

Mary Ellis nodded and Jess swung the front door open, then the screen door inside it. She revealed a quaint single-story house. Every empty surface was covered in porcelain figures of various farm animals and the walls were covered wall to wall with fairly tacky paintings, all wedged together across the walls.

"Wait here, I'm going to go ask my mom if you can stay." Jess rushed from the living room into what Mary Ellis assumed was the kitchen. She could then hear muttering of two different voices, but didn't want to listen, so she busied herself with pacing the edges of the room looking at the various things they had tacked onto the walls.

"Okay, you can come in," Jess yelled after about a minute. Mary Ellis followed her voice into the pastel colored kitchen. On the stove, pork chops were searing in a large pan and the smell was heavenly. In another pan next to it, apples were cooking in cinnamon.

"Hello, Mary Ellis, I'm Linda, Jess's mom." The woman smiled, reaching her hand out to Mary Ellis, who took it.

"Hi." They shook hands and then Linda turned back to the stove, scrambling apples with a spatula.

"Go set the table, Jess," she called over her shoulder.

"Yes, ma'am," Jess giggled and rushed to a drawer near the stove, pulling out four porcelain plates with cow designs on them. Mary Ellis felt both in and out of place standing in the center of the kitchen with nothing to do. She just watched as Jess pulled out a handful of silver forks and steak knives, then red reusable napkins that matched the plates perfectly. Jess piled the utensils into Mary Ellis's arms.

"Come on, let's go." She walked into an adjoining dining room. A chandelier hung over the table, golden light glittering off of the shards of glass. Jess got to work immediately, placing the plates at each of the four seats of the table. Mary Ellis followed behind her, setting out the napkins and utensil.

When they were finished with the table, Jess drifted back into the kitchen with Mary Ellis in tow. Linda told them to go upstairs and clean themselves up before dinner. They headed upstairs to Jess's room, which was painted a sweet shade of lilac. All of the furniture was matching, little lacy details accenting the room. It wasn't at all what Mary Ellis was expecting.

When Jess saw Mary Ellis's face, she blushed.

"My mom wanted a different kind of daughter. It's been like this since I was a baby." She walked over to her closet and opened the door, blocking Mary Ellis's view of her.

"Gran would only act like that when we had to go out together. *I don't want to be seen out with you looking like a little rat,*" Mary Ellis mocked.

Jess giggled.

Mary Ellis was unsure whether she was supposed to change, too. Quickly, she got her answer.

"I can wash your clothes if you want, and give you some to wear while you wait."

"I don't want to-"

"Don't worry about it. I'll give you the really flouncy stuff I hate so I can get rid of them." Jess emerged from the closet in a baseball tee and jean shorts. She squinted at Mary Ellis for a moment, gaging her size and then dove back into the closet. "Just put your clothes in a pile on the floor."

Mary Ellis unzipped her backpack and removed all the dirty clothes from inside, stacking them on the floor. When Jess emerged from the closet once again, she was carrying a pile of clothes. She handed them to Mary Ellis, and turned towards the mirror that hung on the wall over an elaborate white vanity. When Mary Ellis didn't immediately spring into action, she threw a thumb over her shoulder at the closet.

"Go on."

Mary Ellis stepped into the closet and slipped into the slightly oversized pink T-shirt and shorts. When she stepped back into the bed room, Jess was standing in the center of the room with Mary Ellis's clothes in a basket. Mary Ellis lumped her clothes from that day onto the top of the rest of them.

"Thanks," Mary Ellis said.

"It's seriously not a problem. Mom's been begging me to wash my own clothes for weeks now already."

Mary Ellis laughed and they walked downstairs together. While they were loading the washer, the pair heard the door swing open and shut.

"That's my dad," Jess said, "just got home from work." They went out into the dining room, where plates of steaming food were waiting. As they took their seats, Jess's parents slid into the seats across from them.

"I'm David," Jess's father said. He and Mary Ellis shook hands across the table.

The dinner continued without incident, Mary Ellis feeling warm in the family of it all. The meaningless chatter was comforting to her and the food was delicious. She said so multiple times. Somewhere in her heart, Mary Ellis wanted to stay. These people felt more like a family to her after a day, then Gran had in her whole life. Mary Ellis could imagine her life in this town: eating delicious, filling dinners like these every night and finishing them up in a warm bed. Spending her summer days roaming the town with her cluster of friends. She would go to a good school and have lots of people who loved her. Deep down though, Mary Ellis knew she had to go; she would never be completely at home here. When dinner was finished, Mary Ellis thanked Linda and David and went to wait in Jess's room while Jess talked to her father. Mary Ellis settled on the edge of Jess's bed. She knew she should be worried: how easily Jess's parents could call the police and have her sent back home. There was something about them that made Mary Ellis feel they would not though. Maybe it was just the evening that she had had, the filling meal, the ice cream, that created the feeling, but Mary Ellis thought it was something deeper, an understanding of her.

"Mary Ellis, come on down," Jess yelled.

Mary Ellis stood up from the bed and walked down the stairs, heart thumping in her chest. She stepped into the living room, where Jess was sitting in a large cushy armchair, her parents across from her on a loveseat.

"Honey, sit down," Linda pointed at a seat next to the one that Jess was sitting in. Mary Ellis looked from parent to parent, searching their eyes for a hint of whether they would take her. Linda and David looked at each other, then back at Mary Ellis.

"We have a couple of questions for you if that's okay?" Mary Ellis nodded.

"Does your mother or father know that you're coming?" Mary Ellis paused, considering.

"They don't know I'm coming right this moment because I was spending the summer with my grandmother, but I usually stay with them." Mary Ellis folded her hands and placed them in her lap. She stared at her hands, observing each fingernail and the dirt caked underneath.

"Why don't you just call her?"

"I don't know her number off the top of my head." Linda and David exchanged glances and frowned.

"Why didn't you tell the police?"

"I was scared, and now I'm worried that my mom will get in trouble if I call them."

Jess was staring at her feet.

"And the reason why you can't take the bus is because you don't want to run out of money, right?" Mary Ellis nodded. She could feel her heart speed up; the anxiety was starting to get to her.

David turned to Jess.

"Why don't you two go onto the porch? There are popsicles in the freezer that you can have for dessert."

Jess stood up and took Mary Ellis's hand, dragging her back into the kitchen. As soon as they left the room, Jess and Mary Ellis began to hear the parents muttering, too low to hear. Jess retrieved two grape popsicles from the freezer, Mary Ellis's least favorite flavor, but she couldn't complain. Jess walked onto the porch with Mary Ellis following close behind.

The front porch was barren except for a wooden porch swing that was held up by two rusted chains. Jess gestured for Mary Ellis to sit down and when she did, handed her a popsicle. Then Jess sat down on the other side of the swing, lifting her feet up so they rested on Mary Ellis's lap. They both took the white plastic wrapping off of their popsicles and Jess collected the wrappers in her hand. When Mary Ellis handed Jess her wrapper, Jess tucked them into her pocket. Jess sighed and stared off in the distance, sucking on her popsicle.

After a long period of silence, Jess said, "Why did you lie to them?"

"I had to. They wouldn't have helped if I told the truth. They would have called the police. They still might."

Jess frowned. "I still don't think you should lie about it. Maybe you should go into the foster care system if that's what your parents think is best for you."

"Sometimes you have to lie to get what you want. Sometimes you know what's best for yourself."

"You're just a kid," Jess said. She had finished her popsicle, shoving its stick into the jumble of plastic.

"So are you."

Jess peered at her, turning over so she could see Mary Ellis more clearly.

"And I'm not trying to hitchhike down the coast alone."

"Whatever," Mary Ellis said, following Jess's lead she threw her popsicle stick.

"We should go back inside, my parents are probably waiting for us." Jess pulled her feet forward onto the floor and stood up.

"Listen, I'm sorry. You've been nice to me for the whole day and I don't want to make you mad, but you don't understand what I've been through, what I'm going through."

Jess stared at her, then at the floor.

"Sorry." Mary Ellis smiled.

"It's all good." Jess was smiling again too.

"We should probably still go in though, hear their verdict." Jess squinted, mocking seriousness. Mary Ellis nodded, and together they walked inside.

As they opened the door, David rushed up to Mary Ellis, guiding her back into the living room.

"You're going to stay the night tonight. Tomorrow I will drive to the address you have for your parents. We'll make sure you can get as far as you need to. Is that all alright with you?" David peered into Mary Ellis's eyes.

"Thank you," Mary Ellis said, wanting to reach her arms around David's waist and pull him into a hug. Wanting to dance. There would be no more late nights. No more fear of the police or evenings spent wondering whether she would be able to find something to eat. Soon. So soon. Mary Ellis would be with her mother and father once again. They would live a life like this, Mary Ellis wouldn't have to rely on others for the experience of a happy home. She would feel nearly whole like she did here with Linda, David, and Jess.

"You're welcome. We're happy to help, though I'd advise you memorize your parent's number for the future."

"I will. I promise I will." Mary Ellis blinked back tears.

"Now you two should get ready for bed, it's late," Linda called, entering the room from the kitchen. She wore a tired smile.

"I guess you're sleeping over," Jess said. They went upstairs and, as Jess made Mary Ellis a bed on the floor, Mary Ellis brushed her teeth for the first time in several days. She washed her face and combed through her hair. When Mary Ellis was ready for bed, she walked back into the bedroom.

"How could you stand my breath."

"It was alright." Jess smiled. Mary Ellis didn't say anything. "Just tuck in. I have to go brush my teeth be right back."

Mary Ellis turned off the light and climbed into her makeshift bed. She pulled the thick blanket over her shoulders and closed her eyes. After a few minutes, Jess returned and climbed into her own bed, becoming a part of the pile of lilac pillows.

"Goodnight," Mary Ellis said quietly, "I had a great day. Thank you."

"Me too. Night."

Mary Ellis slept peacefully that night. She dreamed of life in the golden heart of North Carolina.

Chapter Twelve

When Stacy had called Leah, asking her if she wanted to come to see a movie with her, she had seemed overjoyed. They'd met up in the center of town; Stacy had come half an hour early and was standing in the corner of the bookstore, holding a book up to her face but keeping her eyes locked on the door. Each time the door open she would jolt, ready to jog forward and pretend that she hadn't been standing there for too long a time, aware that the cashier was watching her as he stood at the counter, clearly irritated with her presence. When, finally, Leah waltzed into the room, Stacy barely glanced up at her, having long since faded into the story of the novel and out of reality.

"Stacy?" Leah had to say, the same as when they first met, to get her to look up and realize that Leah was standing right in front of her.

"Sorry," Stacy mumbled. She blushed nervously, tucking the book back into its place on the shelf.

"Do you want to walk around for a little bit?" Leah asked; it seemed as if she was trying to hold her body to the ground, to keep her limbs from moving against her will.

"Sure," Stacy said, and the started a circuit around the small bookstore, barely glancing at the shelves around them.

"What were you reading?"

"It was just..." Stacy started, but suddenly found herself unable to recall anything from the story she was just so enveloped in, "a story."

Leah laughed, then, trying to pull herself together, said, "I'm sorry."

"You don't need to apologize. I was being stupid."

They'd arrived back at the front of the bookstore and, seeing that neither of them were actually paying attention to their surroundings, stepped out onto the street. They strolled down the town's main street, the summer air heavy with humidity. Leah was wearing a tank top and shorts, looking slightly more put together than Mary Ellis once would have, always in mismatched outfits, T-shirts that didn't quite fit. When Stacy's mind began to wander to thoughts of Mary Ellis, Stacy tried to stop them, she ought to be here, she was sure that Leah was saying something that she'd be expected to respond to, but all she could think about was that she wouldn't be here had Mary Ellis stayed. Wasn't she having fun? This should have been a good time, but Stacy could only think how much easier it would be for her to just go home and sit in her room. To think about better memories in better times and feel heavy with the weight of loss. Instead, she tried to pull herself back to this moment, to the person beside her.

When Stacy checked her phone, she realized it was almost time for the movie she wanted to see to start. "Do you think we should head to the movie now?" Stacy asked finally, turning to face Leah for the first time since they had left the store. Leah made a face and suddenly Stacy was worried that she had just cut her off.

"The next showing of *The Final Force* doesn't start for a half hour." Leah looked at her watch.

Stacy wasn't expecting to see *The Final Force*; it was a spy thriller and had been panned. Stacy wanted to see the latest rom-com, she'd even checked in the paper to make sure it had gotten good reviews, but Leah wanted to do it so she said, "Okay."

They continued down the street, now talking to each other about the little things they had to contend with. They discussed what they were planning to do for the summer – Stacy had nothing planned, but Leah discussed the vacations her parents were going on to the beach and to the Grand Canyon – things they had watched on television recently, books they liked, what they were worried about for middle school. Finally, the time arrived and they headed back to the movie theater, arriving just in time to scoot into their seats during the movie's opening scene. It was a thriller that was apparently based on a book, which Stacy had never read, but Leah had suggested. As they walked out onto the street when the movie was over Leah excitedly detailed the differences between the book and the movie, and what she thought about it. Stacy just nodded along, feeling herself drift away from the conversation as it began.

Eventually, they broke away from each other and Stacy began the walk home, drifting in an airy fog. She guessed she had enjoyed herself; she thought she was happy, at least Leah had seemed to be for nearly the entire day, but something seemed wrong. This wasn't what she imagined in a new friend, it felt more like she was trying to fit someone new into the hole that Mary Ellis had left in her. Leah wasn't the perfect size. Maybe this was Stacy's fault, she needed to stop comparing them and start completely clean, but that wasn't how her mind seemed to work.

Still Stacy wanted to be friends with Leah. She wanted life to feel normal again, even for just a moment. Though she wished that she could feel this way with Mary Ellis. Mary Ellis was gone. She'd have to make her own normal now.

Chapter Thirteen

Mary Ellis was shaken awake by Jess, who was already dressed. In a daze, Mary Ellis stumbled to the bathroom and changed, quickly getting ready by brushing her teeth and hair and snipping the pieces of hair that stuck out with the pair of scissors found in the cabinet above the sink. They were tiny, usually used for clipping hangnails and loose skin, but Mary Ellis figured with a little effort she could keep herself in good shape.

When she was cleaned up, Mary Ellis smiled into the mirror. She had put on the best clothes she had brought with her and thought she now looked halfway decent. She wanted to be as cute and charming as she possibly could.

When she was finished, Mary Ellis walked downstairs to see a breakfast of pancakes and bacon set out on the dining room table. She wanted to cry. It had been so long since Mary Ellis had had pancakes, and the smell wafted over her in waves, enveloping her in sweetness and warmth. She took her seat at the table where Linda and David were already seated and moments later, Jess sprinted into her chair.

"Good morning, ladies," Linda chimed. She began eating when everyone was seated. The others at the table seemed to take her lead and dove into their plates as well.

"Morning, Mom, Dad," Jess said, while Mary Ellis just nodded at them.

"We're going to leave as soon as breakfast is over," David started, his eyes turning to her. "You don't have anything you need to pack, do you?"

"No," Mary Ellis said, and the topic of her leaving wasn't mentioned for the rest of the breakfast. Once again, Mary Ellis felt like she was a real part of the family. They were chatting about what Jess was going to do that day and where Linda was going to get groceries and how David had a big project coming up that he needed to work on when he got back. It all felt so normal. Mary Ellis was leaned over the table by the end of the breakfast, happily sharing her opinions on everything that came up at the table or just listening to the others talk. When the conversation was winding to a close, David stood up from the table.

"Mary Ellis, go get your bags."

He waved her away from the table and so she went, trying to force herself to be ready to leave. Mary Ellis felt herself tearing away from these people already. She had begun to think of them as friends, almost family, but Mary Ellis knew she had known these people for only a day. Soon they would be nothing but a distant memory to her and she would fade away in their minds until they couldn't even remember her name. Mary Ellis had to press on anyway. She walked into Jess's bedroom, grabbed her bags, and hurried out, leaving the bed she'd slept in last night in a pile on the floor.

As Mary Ellis walked down the family's steep stairwell. She watched as Linda and David stood by the doorway. David was slipping on his shoes and then a large, brown leather jacket. It seemed a bit too roguish for him and was too hot for it, but it made Mary Ellis smile. Linda had busied herself with picking up Mary Ellis's shoes and ensuring that they were ready for her when she came downstairs. Jess was nowhere to be found.

Mary Ellis reached the bottom of the stairs and slipped her shoes onto her feet. Then she looked up at the wide face of David, who was staring down at her.

"Jess," he yelled, breaking the eye contact.

"Give me a second."

So they waited. They stood in silence, all wedged in by the door. When Jess entered carrying a duffle bag, David and Linda immediately started to move.

"What are you doing?" Linda asked, watching as Jess strode across the living room.

"Getting ready to go," Jess said, beginning to slip on her shoes.

"But honey," Linda said, placing a hand on Jess's shoulder, "you have swim lessons tomorrow."

Jess groaned and stuck out her bottom lip, dropping the shoe she was slipping on.

"You're not going to miss it just because you want to go on a roadtrip."

"But, Mom," Jess started.

"No but, now go say goodbye to Mary Ellis." With that, Linda turned to Mary Ellis.

"I'm going to wait in the car," David said, leaning down to kiss Linda on the cheek. "See you, honey." He called out to Jess. Linda reached down and squeezed Mary Ellis's shoulder.

"It was lovely to have you here."

"Thank you so much," Mary Ellis said, breathless. A smile broke across Linda's face and she leaned down to give Mary Ellis a real hug. Jess sprinted into the room and pulled

Mary Ellis into more of a bear hug. She held Mary Ellis tightly for a moment and while she was, pressed a small piece of paper into Mary Ellis's hand.

"Call," she whispered. Mary Ellis shoved the paper deep into her pocket and smiled.

"Thank you." Mary Ellis squeezed Jess's hand. Then they separated.

"I had fun."

"Alright, it's time to go now," Linda said, guiding Mary Ellis out the door into the crisp air. There was a slight breeze.

David leaned over and opened the door for Mary Ellis as she walked down the porch stairs and across the yard into the driveway. Mary Ellis started towards the backseat but when she reached it, David raised his eyebrows at her.

"Up front." He said simply, and Mary Ellis blushed. She was more of a kid than she realized. Mary Ellis slipped into the passenger side door. She placed her backpack first at her feet. Then she lifted it into the backseat.

"You ready to go?" Mary Ellis nodded. The car rumbled to life and pulled out of the driveway, crunching on the rocks that it was paved with. As they started down Jess's street, Mary Ellis craned her neck to watch first the house speed out of view and then the street. They bumped across the river and in what seemed like an instant, the whole town was behind them. They were speeding down the highway once again, there was nothing beautiful about the landscape anymore.

Mary Ellis faced forward in her seat and quickly the pair fell into silence. Mary Ellis placed her head against the window of the car and tried to avoid thinking about how quickly the meeting with her family was approaching. Her stomach ached with a mix of anxiety and excitement. She knew her parents would love her, they had to. Mary Ellis squeezed her eyes shut to avoid the landscapes almost dizzying effects as it sped by. She should be excited. Deep breaths.

There was little conversation in the first few hours of their trip. At some point David turned the radio on, singing in a hushed voice to the music on the top 40 station. Mary Ellis thought she fell asleep at one point, fading back into consciousness some time later with only the crust in the corners of her eye and the slight film on her teeth as evidence of her nap. When she was fully awake, Mary Ellis shuffled into an upward position and stared out of the window once again. The nervous coiling of her stomach had calmed, but the excitement had dulled as well. Now it was just a wait. After a few minutes, Mary Ellis began to feel eyes on the side of her face. David's eyes. She turned towards him, meeting his eyes and smiled. He turned back towards the road, but smiled back.

"Are you sure your parents are going to be home when we get there? I can wait with you if you need to make sure."

"I'm sure they'll be there. If not, I can wait by myself, I know the area." A grin, a real grin, spread across Mary Ellis's face and she watched David as he guided the car along the highway. The sun hung low, coloring the sky with a blaze of orange. Mary Ellis guessed they would be stopping soon. She leaned back in her seat.

"Are you sure?"

"Yeah, of course. I'll be fine I promise."

David cast another glance at her. Mary Ellis suddenly seemed small in the seat under his gaze.

"It'd really be no trouble to wait with you," David said. Mary Ellis laughed.

"Whatever you want."

The car then fell silent. David was watching the side of the road, seemingly looking for a place to stop.

"Thank you," Mary Ellis whispered, "I was having a really hard time before Jess found me. Even just seeing your family was wonderful. You all seem so happy."

"We're happy to help you. Really." Another pause. "I wish you would tell us everything that was happening to you."

"I can't. I really can't."

"We wouldn't laugh or hurt you or whatever you think is going to happen."

"I'm sorry."

"It's alright. I know I should have called the police, make sure you get to the place you need to go and I know this probably seems like I'm just trying to get you out of my hands as soon as possible, but I'm not."

"I understand."

"I just want to help you and this seems like the way to help."

David was easing his way into the parking lot of a quaint restaurant.

"Trust me, I understand, you've done enough already."

The car pulled into a space next to the restaurant's door. David began to climb out of the car and Mary Ellis followed him. The restaurant was a small white paneled building that looked almost like it could be somebody's home. Moss was coiled around the columns that held up a sagging porch. As they walked across the porch the boards creaked underneath their feet. David pulled open the screen door of the house and held it open, letting Mary Ellis slip underneath his arm. Mary Ellis walked down the hall with David in tow and stepped into the small dining room. David walked up to the small podium, where a hostess was standing. Mary Ellis just stood at the mouth of the dining room, glancing around at all parts of it.

There were only a few rickety tables in the dining room, but the ceilings were high and a chandelier was perched in the center of the room, light glittering off of the tiny shards of glass. Mary Ellis took a stunned step towards the table closest to her. David grabbed her shoulder and Mary Ellis stopped, turning towards a table in the corner of the room. She sat down gently onto the seat. Mary Ellis couldn't tell whether she thought the room was pretty or not. Either way it was captivating. She was stunned by it.

A waitress approached their table, placing two large menus onto its waxy surface. She smiled and nodded at them.

"Can I get you all anything to drink?" They ordered drinks. Mary Ellis got Sprite, she hadn't had it in a long time. The woman hustled away from the table back to the kitchen, which Mary Ellis could see into slightly from the place where she was sitting. Just more low light and people rushing around. She could smell something wonderful wafting through the air, slightly meaty and heavily spiced. Mary Ellis's eye broke away from the kitchen and turned to the menu. All of the food available seemed to be comfort food, except for a few things that Mary Ellis had never heard of. She and David sat in silence until the waitress returned to take their orders. Mary Ellis ordered a tortellini soup.

When the waitress stepped away from the table, taking the menus with her, there was nothing left to do.

"We're heading to a bed and breakfast the hostess recommended to me when we were talking. Tomorrow I'll drive you down as far as we can get, I think we might be able to make it to your parents' house. That alright?" David muttered, almost to himself.

"Yeah."

"I know it is probably hard for you to-"

"Just stop, please." Mary Ellis blushed, staring down into her lap. The hum of the kitchen and the quaint buzz of the dining room wasn't anything normal for Mary Ellis, but she could pretend like it was if she tried really hard. If she squeezed her eyes shut she could imagine her mother's young face sitting across from her at the table, her dark hair just brushing her shoulders. Her father is squeezed in next to her mother, his arm threaded around her waist, new stubble just forming on his cheeks making them scratchy when Mary Ellis kissed them. When her eyes opened though, it was just David.

"Sorry," she said eventually, not breaking eye contact with her lap.

"Can I say just one more thing about it?" David asked, holding up his hand gently. Mary Ellis nodded. "You know that if you're ever in danger, if you ever need somewhere to stay, Linda and I would be happy to help you in any way that we can."

"You've been more than enough help to me already."

"Just keep that in mind." David's fingers rapped the table, he glanced around the room. "I'll give you our number."

"Jess already did." Mary Ellis pulled the crumpled piece of paper out of her pocket and spread it on the table. David smiled.

"Here, let me just give you our address too." He slid the piece of paper across the table towards him and then went fishing in a briefcase he had brought with him. Removing a pen from one of the side pockets, David scribbled the family's address in a scrawl that Mary Ellis could just barely make out. He then slid it back to her. Mary Ellis stared at it for only a moment before stuffing it back into her bag.

With that the dinner lapsed into another relative silence. When the food was brought to the table, the pair abandoned all hope of talking, instead just eating hungrily. Though at first the soup burned Mary Ellis's tongue, it created a warmth in her stomach that, to be fair, was probably a bit uncomfortable for the summer heat, but Mary Ellis didn't care. It spread through all her limbs reaching the very tips of her fingers with a comfort she barely recognized from home. The bright orange mac-and-cheese that Gran had always made for her almost gave her the same feeling, though this tasted so much better. The sudden remembrance of the feeling brought Mary Ellis back home for just a moment. That first day when Gran was standing over her, telling her about what the rest of her life would be like. Gran was gone. Now it was up to Mary Ellis to make her own future. She was deciding what her life would be like from now on. Gran is gone. Mary Ellis whispered the thought to herself, reveling in the truth of it. What a strange truth it was. And what a strange truth that Gran's disappearance stirred little emotion in her except for an almost guilty elation that leapt in the pit of her stomach.

Mary Ellis pushed it down, down, down until she felt nothing at all. Then David was paying the bill and tapping on her hand and they were leaving the restaurant. Out in the parking lot, Mary Ellis clambered into the car and they drove down the road for a little while, exhaustion was slipping into Mary Ellis's bones. In a moment, Mary Ellis was walking into the bed and breakfast. She was in a daze. She was outside herself. Mary Ellis was watching David get a room and then following him upstairs. He took too long opening up the door and Mary Ellis barely took it in before she was burying her face into the pillow and pulling the blankets around her head. David was saying something to her, but all Mary Ellis could think about was sleep. She couldn't even find it in herself to say anything except goodnight.

"Good night," she said, her mind's spin starting to slow. Good night. Good night. Good night. David was saying something else. Mary Ellis mashed her eyes shut. The room was hot and the bedding was itchy. Sleep came quickly just the same.

Chapter Fourteen

It had been four days since Stacy had missed Mary Ellis's call. Since then, Stacy had stayed inside her home all day, not willing to let her phone be unplugged from the wall. Leah had called a few times, sending Stacy hurtling towards her phone from where ever else she was in the room. Even when she was almost sure that it wouldn't be Mary Ellis, Stacy would still answer the phone with a hushed, "hello," and then hurry to end the call.

When it was Leah who called, Stacy would entertain her with conversation for a few minutes before shutting her down, claiming that her parents were calling her or that she had somewhere else she needed to be. Stacy couldn't tell whether she wanted Leah to keep calling or not. She enjoyed the banality of Leah's small talk, the way she would always steer the conversation with her own interests. This allowed Stacy to drift off into her own thoughts, to consider what she wanted without having to worry about what she was going to say to Mary Ellis when she inevitably called. Stacy suspected that eventually Leah would assume she was just being blown off and stop calling, but Stacy might have been okay with that as well, she was just letting whatever happened happen. Stacy couldn't go back to the comic book store or on a hike or out to lunch.

On the fifth day though, Stacy began to feel a rising frustration at Mary Ellis, Leah, everyone. She wished that Leah would ask her what she wanted to do or invite herself over to Stacy's house, so that Stacy could be with both Mary Ellis and Leah at once. She wished Mary Ellis would just call, so Stacy could fulfil her duties to her and continue on with her life. She wished her parents would quit just skirting around her, acting like this wasn't what they expected that she'd be doing this summer now that Mary Ellis was gone.

Most of all, Stacy was frustrated with herself and her inability to unravel all of the strings of her life into something more easy to parse out. She wanted to forget Mary Ellis and the worry she felt towards her. She wanted to spend more time with Leah, but assert her own will over the situation and invite Leah over. To tell her what she wanted to do. Still, Stacy was tangled in her anxieties, so she stayed stuck to her phone, stuck to her home.

That was until Leah called that afternoon. "Stacy?" she asked the moment that Stacy picked up the phone, slightly out of breath.

For a moment, Stacy was floored. Usually Leah greeted her in a flurry of small talk or by nearly shouting out a fully formed plan, but this time the short greeting was all. Stacy was sure that it was going to be Mary Ellis, it almost sounded like her voice, but then Leah continued on.

"I was thinking that we could go to the mall over in New Haven. My mom could give us a ride."

Everything inside of Stacy came loose. She realized waiting by the phone wasn't doing any good; Mary Ellis would never call with her right there. Still, she didn't really want to go to the mall, even though it'd probably be good for her to get out.

"Actually, I think we should go to the bowling alley out across the highway. I'll meet you there if you're in."

Leah paused for a moment. "Alright."

"See you in like half an hour?"

"Sure," Leah replied.

This time Stacy was first to hang up the phone.

***

Stacy waved her parents off as she left the house, a couple of dollars shoved into the pocket of her jean shorts. Stacy retraced the steps she'd taken that day to the highway, the sun beating down on her. By the time she reached the highway once again, her skin was glistening with sweat and her hair clung to her forehead and the back of her neck. As she peered across the traffic at the bowling alley, waiting for the perfect moment to cross, Stacy was pricked at once with fear of missing Mary Ellis's call. If she hasn't called in five days, she reasoned, she probably wouldn't be calling now, but Stacy could never be sure.

For a moment she considered heading home again, but right as that thought crossed her mind, the traffic parted, leaving her with the perfect spot to cross the highway. Barely thinking, Stacy began to sprint, dashing out into traffic and onto the median that separated the two directions of traffic. Adrenaline rushed through her veins as she waited for the next gap in traffic, holding her hand against her forehead to block the sun from her eyes. When it came, Stacy sprinted the rest of the way, ending up in the bowling alley's parking lot. She took a passing glance at the valley below, pushing all thoughts of Mary Ellis and wherever she may have gone out of her mind. Plastering a smile on her face, Stacy pushed her way into the bowling alley, scanning the lobby for Leah, her hand still clutched around her phone. Just in case.

Chapter Fifteen

Mary Ellis woke up disoriented. She was in a strange room that seemed to be coated in dust, with thick curtains hanging from a small window at one side of it that had been nudged slightly open. Two heavy, full beds with brass frames sat side by side in the bedroom. David was standing next to the bed, muttering to someone on the phone that was seated on the bedside table that sat between the two beds. It all came rushing back into her head. The bed and breakfast.

"It's almost time for breakfast," David said simply, already dressed, "then we're going to head out."

Mary Ellis sat up and blinked, shaking the sleep from her eyes.

"Are you okay?" David asked.

"Yeah, I'm fine. I'm just going to get dressed."

"You sure? You were acting kind of strangely last night."

Mary Ellis nodded.

"I was just thinking about some stuff."

"Feel free to talk if you need to." The smile on David's face seemed so earnest.

"I will," Mary Ellis said quietly, though she had no plans to. Instead, Mary Ellis picked up her bags and headed to the bathroom. She didn't have time to shower, but she could still make herself look presentable. "Soon" she said to herself, trying to smile like she would when she met them. As she combed through her hair and tried her hardest to uncrease her nicest shirt, Mary Ellis repeated this fact to herself several times.

Her heart pricking with nostalgia, Mary Ellis swore to herself she would call Stacy the moment she got the opportunity, but for right now she'd have to settle with reading over her parents' letter, knowing she'd be with them soon.

She searched through each and every bag, emptying her things all over the floor. When each crevice was checked and Mary Ellis knew that her thick sheath of birthday cards wasn't inside, she collapsed on the ground. Wanting to cry, Mary Ellis squeezed her eyes shut. *Soon enough. Soon enough. Soon enough.* She wouldn't need the cards because her real parents would be there to hold her. As calmly as she could manage, Mary Ellis walked back into the bedroom. She began to search for the birthday cards. She peeked under the bed, crouched on her hands and knees, tore all of the bedding off the bed, and opened every drawer that was in the dresser even though she hadn't opened any of them the night before.

"What are you looking for?" David asked, staring down at her from across the room.

Mary Ellis sank back into a seated position and looked up at him.

"I had all these old birthday cards that my parents gave me. I haven't taken it out in a while so I don't know where it could be." She turned back to her work, crawling around on the floor and beginning to peer under everything. David began to help without another word. He searched through his own bed and in the closet, even going into the bathroom to look again in there.

"We need to go downstairs to get breakfast or we're going to miss it." David was standing right above her.

"It's gone," Mary Ellis said. She felt, empty, untethered. A tear ran down her cheek, but Mary Ellis swept it away.

"You'll see your parents soon. You won't need the cards."

Mary Ellis wanted to beg and plead for them to stay a little longer, to take another look, but she knew there was no use. She stood up and followed David out of their room. He stared down at her.

"Don't worry," he whispered to her. The words only stirred Mary Ellis's stomach.

At breakfast, Mary Ellis didn't feel much better. As she ate her food, David spent the time chatting to the hostess with a wiry white bun and her husband, a man with a pipe dangling out of his mouth that he wasn't smoking. Mary Ellis could only wrack her brain for other places she could have left the cards. They could have come tumbling out of her bag when Charles ripped it away from her or when she was running through the woods or one of the many times she had changed clothes since she had left for the trip. She was itching to go back upstairs and just look a little longer, but Mary Ellis stayed glued to the table. She was completely wrapped in her own thoughts. Nobody said anything to her.

When breakfast was over, David and Mary Ellis loaded back into the car. Though Mary Ellis's thoughts were still turned towards the cards. What if she didn't recognize the people who came to get her and she needed to make sure that it was her parents? No, she would remember her mother's dark hair and matching eyes and the way her cheeks were always spotted with freckles and her father's stubble and his long, long legs that always towered over Mary Ellis and the way his hair always hung slightly longer than her mother's and her father would let Mary Ellis braid it on occasion, grinning as she wove the strands together. What if her parents didn't remember her? Mary Ellis stared down at herself, a wave of anxiety passing over her. She looked so different, was so much bigger, than she had been when she had last seen her.

At last Mary Ellis touched one of her back pockets only to find a single folded paper inside. One of the more recent birthday cards. Though it was completely alone, Mary Ellis figured that at least she had something to prove to her parents that she was theirs. Inside all that was scribbled was 'Love you lots M.E.! We're so happy to hear about how big you're getting. XO Mom and Dad.' Mary Ellis repeated this to herself a few times, trying to memorize it. She knew that she could never replace the letters she'd lost, but hopefully she would see her parents soon enough.

This was pretty much how the rest of the ride went. Mary Ellis was so enveloped in herself that she didn't realize when the air became balmy and hot. She barely realized when David, who had been checking the map much more in the last hour, pulled to a stop in a wide parking lot. She only came crashing back into her head when David asked her to get out of the car.

When Mary Ellis stepped out of the car, the first thing she noticed was the thick, heat. A wash of calm rushed over her. It only lasted a moment though before Mary Ellis realized where she was. Directly in front of her was a skinny, grey apartment complex. It looked a bit dingier than Mary Ellis remembered, the cement siding chipped in some places and the fence that surrounded the complex's tiny yard was falling apart in places. But this was it. Her home.

While David busied himself with the car, Mary Ellis looked up and down the street. She wasn't sure what she was expecting it to look like, but this wasn't it. A bus terminal was directly next to the house. Two buildings down was a 7-11 and beyond that Mary Ellis could see a pawn shop. Unlike Gran's neighborhood, there were few things that Mary Ellis could recognize as houses around. She frowned.

"You ready?" he asked, holding Mary Ellis's bags out to her.

She nodded. "I think I should go up alone."

David frowned.

"I don't know if that's-"

"I wouldn't want my parents to think that you took me or hurt me or something." Mary Ellis stared at a point behind David. The building across the street was a grocery store. If she looked closely, Mary Ellis could tell what was in the windows.

"I really don't think they'd think that."

"I just don't want you to come up with me. I want everything to be normal again."

David furrowed his brow for a moment, considering Mary Ellis. "And you're sure you'll be alright?"

"Positive." Mary Ellis nodded as she spoke.

David sighed. "Okay then."

Mary Ellis smiled as softly as she could at him then and adjusted the bags on her shoulders. She watched as David climbed back into the car and waited.

"I want to make sure you get inside," he said.

Mary Ellis's smile didn't waver.

"Goodbye," Mary Ellis said, waving.

"Call us when you get settled, alright?"

"Alright."

"See you later, kid."

Mary Ellis turned from David's car and heard the motor starting. She walked towards the building, trying her hardest to remain confident that this was normal, hoping that David would drive off.

As she approached the door to the complex, Mary Ellis kept her ears alert, she could still hear the car idling behind her. Once more she turned.

"Thank you," she said to David, smiling widely at him. She was sure it looked fake.

"It was no trouble," he smiled.

With that, Mary Ellis pushed the door open and pressed her way into the apartment complex's lobby. She heard the car roar away. She was alone. For a moment Mary Ellis took in the view of the lobby. It was a cramped space with one wall overtaken by rows of mailboxes, stairs snaked up the opposite wall, it couldn't have been more than five steps between them. Everything here seemed so much more cold and unfamiliar than she remembered. Mary Ellis stared at the stairs, suddenly dreading the walk up them.

She lingered for what felt like a long time, until she heard someone's footsteps on the stair. Mary Ellis jolted and rushed out of the building, fear flooding through her.

Mary Ellis sank down onto the bus bench along the almost deserted sidewalk. The sun was just above the horizon. It seemed almost taunting to her. *Coward*, it said, *time keeps passing and yet you are doing nothing but sitting on your ass*.

Indignant, Mary Ellis curled herself onto the bus bench and retrieved a book from her backpack. A Nancy Drew. She tried her hardest to sink into the story, just to pass some time before she felt confident enough to walk upstairs, but her thoughts were pulled to Stacy. They used to play Nancy Drew together. Stacy would be Nancy and Mary Ellis would be a murderer and she would hide. When Stacy would find her, Mary Ellis would pop out and pretend to murder her

133

in increasingly violent ways. That got them sent to time out more than a couple of times.

Mary Ellis almost laughed she remembered a time when time outs would make her shake with anxiety for what was to come. When she could be threatened by a phone call to Gran. Now Mary Ellis was in control of everything, she had no reason to fear. Mary Ellis was here. She was home. Besides, she really needed to use the restroom. Maybe she'd just call Stacy first though, it would be nice to share how close she was with someone.

Chapter Sixteen

Stacy was just passing through the kitchen, about to head out the door, her phone began ringing in her pocket. Stacy felt something near electricity run down her spine. It rang again. She glanced around the room, ensuring her parents weren't anywhere to be found, before pressing the phone to her ear.

"Stacy?" The voice was small, just like hers, and sounded tired, but almost excited at the same time. Stacy felt all the breath rush out of her.

"Mary Ellis?" Stacy whispered.

Mary Ellis laughed.

"Yeah, it's me." Stacy heard something like a car pass by on Mary Ellis's side of the line.

"Where are you?"

"I'm in North Carolina at a bus stop. I'm right outside of my house."

Stacy's heart sank. Anxiously, she fiddled with the things in her pockets.

"Oh. Nice." Silence lingered for a moment.

"So how is it back home?" Stacy glanced around her house, everything seemed still and silent, not even birds seemed to be making a sound. Stacy's things from school and trips with Leah were strewn about the room, but there was no sign of anything but routine.

"I've been doing a lot, going out on my own. I keep seeing movies-"

"Cool." Another pause.

"Is anyone worried about me?" The tone of Mary Ellis's voice gave Stacy pause. There was something almost eager about the way she asked.

"Yeah, everyone is. The police talked to me about you."

"What did you tell them?"

Mary Ellis should have been more scared, at least nervous. Stacy had had to lie for her, lie to the police. She'd had to worry for ages, to spend too much time thinking about where Mary Ellis would be at this very moment. She had had to be afraid. But Mary Ellis was too calm. Everything seemed too easy.

Stacy sighed.

"Mary, they probably think you're dead." For the next few seconds all Stacy heard was strange, almost surprised sounds.

"You told them I was dead?"

"No, no. You've just been gone for so long-"

"You didn't tell them where I was, right?"

"I...I..."

"I'm about to see my mom, Stacy, if they come and get me-"

"I told you, they think you're dead," Stacy nearly yelled, then clasped her hand over her mouth.

"Good." There was a long moment.

"Sorry," Mary Ellis said just as a similar sorry burst out of Stacy's mouth. Stacy didn't know what to say anymore. This used to be so easy. Everything used to be so easy.

"This is weird," Mary Ellis said eventually, and Stacy smiled.

"Yeah." Stacy crushed the money she had with her into a tight ball as she closed and opened her fist. "It's just been hard, missing you and everything." Stacy felt heat rush to her cheeks.

"It's been hard for me too. In different ways." Stacy could hear a new warmth in Mary Ellis's voice. "Not that I didn't miss you too."

"So, you found your parents?" Stacy asked after a moment.

"Finally. All I have to do is walk right up the stairs and knock on their door." Mary Ellis exhaled, shakily.

"Are you nervous?" Stacy tried to tread lightly, Mary Ellis wasn't exactly known for her level-headedness.

"I think so."

"I wish I could help you."

Mary Ellis's voice came out strained. "I wish you could too." A beat. "Everything going good for you?"

"I met this girl Leah. She's really nice but I don't know if you'd like her. She's kind of excitable."

"Good for you." There was a hint of jealousy in her voice. "I'm sorry I- shit-"

Stacy heard a loud beep that sounded like it came from the other end of the line.

"My battery is dying. I have to go. Bye."

And then the line went dead. Stacy stood once again in the quiet of her kitchen. All she could hear was the ticking of the clock on the wall across the room and the sound of the house settling. Stacy could imagine where Mary Ellis was right at this moment: standing in the center of a bustling bus terminal, people rushing around her as she clutched onto her backpack, walking powerfully through the street, people parting in her path. Mary Ellis would achieve all she'd wanted, while Stacy was just stuck at home.

Stacy placed the phone back on the hook and walked to the table. Stacy had lost all want to go out. Instead, she found herself plodding back and forth in the kitchen staring into the fridge and opening cabinets, trying to find the will to do something. Instead, her mind wandered. It wandered to the policeman who had once sat with her and Mrs. Kaufman's warnings to the children that if they had any information about Mary Ellis they should tell her. She thought of Mary Ellis once again, but now she was small, just like Stacy. She was alone and cold and scared. She was never coming back. Stacy would have to live without her for the rest of time. Stacy sunk deep into this thought, sinking into a seat at the table. Mary Ellis would never be with her again. They could exchange calls or even texts later, but Stacy somehow knew she would never see her.

The door flew open and Stacy jumped, knocking a pile of junk mail off of the table.

"Hey hon, how was your day?" It was her father, tie hanging loosely around his neck. He dropped his briefcase at the front door and walked to her.

"Fine."

He peered at her for a moment.

"Are you alright? You seem a bit nervous."

She turned around slightly.

"Yeah, Dad, I'm fine."

"I just worry about you. You know, if you ever need to talk about anything I'm here. Alright?"

"I know." Stacy tried to stand, but her father placed his hand on her shoulder, pressing her down into her seat. "Listen, kiddo," he said, sinking down into the seat next to her, "I'm going to be honest with you." Stacy looked up at him, scrunching her face up. "You've been acting really strange recently. Your mother told me that you've been going out a lot. I just need to know where you're going."

"Dad, you don't get it."

"What don't I get?"

"I don't always have time to tell you. I have friends now that sometimes ask me to do things on short notice. Besides, you never cared where I was when Mary Ellis was around."

"You know that her leaving changed-"

"Why should it? I didn't change."

"You did."

"It doesn't matter. She's fi-"

"What?" Her father stopped and turned to face her. "What did you do?"

There was a long stretch of silence.

"I know where she is," Stacy whispered.

"What? Where who is?" Stacy's father's eyes bulged.

"Mary Ellis. She's in North Carolina, looking for her mom."

"Stacy how long have you known?" His voice pitched slightly, but it was clear he was trying to keep from yelling.

Tears began to flow from Stacy's eyes. "I'm sorry. I didn't know what to do."

"You should have told us. You should have told someone."

He walked over to the phone on the other side of the room.

"Why didn't you?"

Stacy stared at her hands, she felt the words blocking her throat. *I thought she would hate me. She's my best friend and I love her and though I want her to be safe, I know she could do this. I know she could get there and I know how badly she wanted it. How frequently she talked about how she wanted to see her parents again or what her normal family would be like. I thought I would lose her, she would hate me when she found out. She wouldn't even speak to me when we got back. I thought you all would hate me when I told you. I know I waited for too long. Everything would be ruined if I told. Don't you understand that everything would have been ruined?*

"I don't know." Stacy sunk down into the table, placing her head in her hands.

"When did you last speak to her?" he asked, his eyes pleading.

"She just called," Stacy whispered

"You're being serious?" His fingers hovered over the numbers on the phone. Stacy nodded. He punched in something that Stacy couldn't see and then pressed the phone to his ear.

"Hi, can I speak to Detective Martin? Yes, it's about the Walker case... Well I've received pertinent information from my daughter... Yes, very important... Alright, thank you." He stared at Stacy from across the room, leaning against the wall. "Hi Detective Martin, do you have a minute to talk? Stacy just revealed to me that she knows where Mary Ellis is.

No, she just told me and I don't have a lot of other information... You are welcome to talk to her right now, she's sitting right here." Stacy's father crossed the kitchen, phone in hand. Stacy watched as the cord stretched all the way until it was completely straight. Her father pressed the phone to her ear. Gingerly, she took it from him.

"Stacy, I'm not going to ask you how long you've known, but you should be aware that withholding information from the police is a crime. If you do this later on it could have serious consequences," Detective Martin began.

Tears welled in Stacy's eyes.

"You could have put your friend in danger by not telling us everything you know, so we need you to tell us everything she told you now.

"Yes," Stacy croaked, the phone shaking in her hand.

"Okay, what do you have to tell me?"

"She's in North Carolina, looking for her mom."

"Do you know for sure that she made it there?" He sounded tense, almost angry. Stacy wanted to sob.

"She just called me to tell me that she made it there."

"Did you get the number she called from? Did she tell you where she was? Where she was going?"

"She just said she was in a bus stop. I'd guess she was going to wherever her mom was staying."

"And you didn't get the number?"

"No. I'm sorry."

"Do you know her mother's name? How she got in contact with her?"

"She said she found her number in the phonebook."

For a moment, Stacy tried to study Detective Martin's voice, she couldn't decide how angry she thought he was.

"Is that all the information you have at this moment?"

"For right now."

"Call us if you have any other information. I hope you understand the severity of withholding this information from us, Stacy."

Stacy just nodded, staring into her lap.

"I'm sorry," she whispered, but Detective Martin said nothing at first.

"Give the phone to your father."

She felt herself slipping up and away, out of her head, barely even hearing as her father returned to the table.

"How could you do this, Stacy?" her father said.

It took a moment for Stacy's head to snap back into focus, and she considered not responding, but decided against it.

"I'm sorry," Stacy mumbled.

"What were you thinking?" Her father didn't seem like he was really looking for an answer.

"I just wanted her to see her mother. She missed her so much."

"She could have gotten killed, Stacy."

"I know," Stacy cried, already bristling, ready for a fight with her father who clearly didn't understand, but he retreated without another word. He didn't get up and walk away, but Stacy could feel him pulling away from her.

"Dad," Stacy said, more forcefully than she intended.

All that her father mustered was a meek, "Honey."

"I'm going to go upstairs." Her father just sighed. For once, Stacy wished he would punish her. She wished that he would scream and call her mother down and that they would yell at her as they sat on opposite sides of the table. She had done what was objectively the worst thing in her entire life, but nobody cared. Her mother just sat up in their bedroom or went out with friends, while her father gave up. He was pitiful.

Stacy stood up from the table and stared down at her father. She wanted to slam her fists and scream "say something. Talk to me." but she turned away from the table and walked upstairs, past her mother's bedroom door and into her bedroom. She sank slowly onto the bed.

She heard her father pad up the stairs and into his bedroom a little while later then she heard him leave the house. A few hours later Stacy heard what she assumed was her mother leaving the house. She wanted to leave her bed and go downstairs, but she didn't have anything to do.

Stacy wished she could talk to Mary Ellis, so she could yell and rant and explain as Mary Ellis would let her do, but the only number she had was for a payphone. Desperate for conversation, Stacy placed a call to the number she had just heard from. The phone rang once, twice, three times, but no one picked up. Stacy felt as if she had nothing left.

Chapter Seventeen

The sun beat down on Mary Ellis's head as she placed the phone back on its hook and surveyed the rest of the street, taking one last look at the street she barely recognized, Mary Ellis turned back towards the building and entered the apartment complex. She pushed into the building and up the stairs, finding herself in an instant in front of her parents' apartment door.

Mary Ellis planted herself in front of the door of apartment 2B, attempting to steel herself against whatever was behind it. She took a few small, shaky breaths, making her hands into fists. Taking one last breath, she squeezed her eyes shut and lifted her hand towards the doorknob. She knocked once, lightly, then stopped. As she began to force herself to knock again, the door slid open, just a crack.

"Hello?"

The woman standing in front of Mary Ellis stood only a tiny bit taller than she, standing slightly slumped over, as if it were an effort to stand. She fondled a piece of her thin, cornflower-blonde hair, blinking her pair of nearly piercing blue eyes blankly at Mary Ellis.

"Rachel?" Mary Ellis stammered, but already her heart felt like it had been crushed, stomped on. The woman in front of her was not her mother.

"I'm sorry I'm not..." The woman's face contorted into a pained grimace. There was a mix of pity and confusion that made Mary Ellis squirm. She was already ignoring the woman though, attempting to figure out how to get out of the situation. As her mind reeled, she peered past the woman into the heart of her apartment. Behind the woman, Mary Ellis could see a corner of the living room. The furniture was all different: a slightly modernized set made of dark wood, but the carpeting and walls remained the same. Mary Ellis could even see a dark purple stain on the pale yellow carpet that matched one she had made years earlier.

***

A faded memory of sitting in the middle of the carpet in the living room, drinking a grape juice. Mary Ellis was absentmindedly playing with a Barbie when her mother and father entered, already yelling.

"We will only need to leave for an hour at most. She can just stay here," her father was saying, grabbing her mother's wrist.

"But it's not safe."

"It's safer than taking her with us-"

"They wouldn't-"

"You think they wouldn't hurt a child? I'm sure they would."

Rachel cast a long glance at Mary Ellis.

"Fine."

The couple began to move towards the door and seeing them, Mary Ellis started to cry. She squeezed her juice box in frustration, sending purple liquid spraying across the floor. Her father just sighed and shut the door behind him, locking Mary Ellis in.

***

The woman shrank away from the doorframe, threatening to slip back behind the door and slam it shut behind her. "I'm not sure you have the right address." Then a pause. "I'm sorry."

Her brow was furrowed with concern, but her voice sounded almost whiny, reluctant. Mary Ellis stood frozen in the doorframe, the woman continued to stare blankly at her, her hands shaking on the doorframe.

"Who are you looking for?" the woman asked, her voice barely audible. Then, "who's Rachel?" Her voice was eternally trailing off.

Mary Ellis faltered.

"My aunt. My mother sent me down to see if she's alright. She hasn't been in contact with her for a little while."

The woman nodded slowly, eventually speeding up. A smile spread across her face.

"Well, she isn't here. She hasn't been here for a while if this ever was her real address. I've lived here for a couple of years." The woman's feet were shifting on the floor, she seemed desperate to slam the door shut.

"Oh...alright."

Another long stretch of silence.

"So you should just tell your mama that."

Mary Ellis nodded.

"Is that all you needed, honey?"

Mary Ellis desperately wanted to come inside. She wanted to slip through the rooms, see where she used to sleep, where her parents used to stay. She wanted to sit on the floor next to the stain and feel like she was a kid again. She took a step towards the woman, who still hadn't told Mary Ellis her name. The woman shrunk back.

"Can I use your bathroom?" Mary Ellis asked in one last, desperate attempt at getting inside, but the woman frowned at her.

"I'm sorry. I don't think that that's a good idea." The woman stood still, watching Mary Ellis with wide eyes, expectantly.

"I'm going to leave now," Mary Ellis said, her voice felt flat. She pulled away from the door and started down the hall. The woman shut the door without another word: Mary Ellis could hear the lock click from down the hall.

When she reached the top of the stairwell, Mary Ellis sank down to the floor, her head swimming. She wasn't sure what else she should do, if her parents had moved on without a trace, she didn't know where else she could find them. A few words haunted her, "I moved in a few years ago." Her heart sank thinking of the letters she received from even months before now written from that address. She would have to go to the library or something, to find out if her parents were somewhere close by.

For a moment, Mary Ellis considered the fact that there was nothing she could do if her parents had left the area: internet research would probably be her best bet for finding them, but the internet could only take her so far. She couldn't stop to think yet or the fear that had flooded her heart would overtake her, she just had to keep moving.

She fled down the stairwell and nearly tumbled out into the street. The streets were almost abandoned: the occasional adult strode down them, but their eyes drifted over her and they continued on their way without incident. She needed to find a library. It was late, so the library would definitely be closed, but she just needed to find it, be ready for tomorrow.

Taking the map out of her pocket, Mary Ellis found the library and started towards it. It didn't take her long to get there, but when she did she was exhausted. She stared at the closed door to the library for a moment, before creeping around the back of the building, where a small parking lot sat next to an even smaller garden. Inside the garden a cluster of benches sat in a circle under a streetlight. Mary Ellis approached one of the benches and lay down, covering her face with a T-shirt to try to block some of the light. For a long while, she just lay there staring up at the sky. The stars seemed to sparkle for her and the sound of the trees rustling provided a comforting sound. Eventually, she fell into sleep.

***

The air was thick with flies as Mary Ellis opened her eyes. Even before her eyes opened she could hear them, the harsh buzz made loud by the sheer number of flies in the room. They alighted on her skin at random, tickling her bare arms and legs. For a moment, Mary Ellis struggle to take in the room, the flies a thick curtain separating her from the world. Slowly though, a space cleared in front of her and Mary Ellis could see. It was Gran's room. Where was Gran?

Standing, Mary Ellis wobbled across the room to the place where she knew the bed to be. It came into her view just as it was when she last saw it. There was a large mass of blankets in the center of the bed.

"Gran?" Mary Ellis said quietly, making her way around the edge of the bed. She wasn't sure why she did it, knowing what she would find when she reached the side of Gran's bed, but Mary Ellis felt compelled to continue forward until she was directly in front of Gran's face.

It was like a movie. Gran's face decaying, bits of flesh sliding off, maggots crawling out of her mouth. Mary Ellis sobbed, reeling from the bed and turning towards the door. Anything to avoid seeing Gran. As she turned, Mary Ellis caught sight of two figures by the door. She screamed, pushing through the blanket of flies to see her mother and father opening the door.

"Help," she screamed.

Her mother glanced at her for a moment, but didn't respond.

"She can just stay here," her father said, already in the hall.

Her mother followed. "But it's not safe."

He shut the door. Mary Ellis heard the door's lock click. She was alone with Gran. Mary Ellis sank down against the door, tucking her head against her knees. She pressed her eyes closed.

***

This time Mary Ellis leapt awake. There was a woman standing over her, a concerned look furrowed into her brow. Her large tortishelle glasses hung close to the edge of her nose, threatening to fall over the edge right onto Mary Ellis.

"What the hell?" Mary Ellis spat, launching herself upwards. The woman jumped back, coming away from her.

"Are you alright?" the woman said. Her voice sounded almost like a prolonged sigh.

"Yeah, I'm fine. I'm just waiting for the library to open." Mary Ellis collected her things off of the bench, ready to run if necessary.

"Have you been here all night?" The woman's messenger bag hung at her side. She quickly pulled it up to her chest when Mary Ellis stood, as if in an act of protection. The creases in her forehead deepened.

"I just got here an hour ago and it wasn't open so I laid down. I guess I fell asleep." The woman then nodded, her face smoothing out until it was smooth as Mary Ellis's own.

"Well, come on then." The woman dropped her messenger bag back to her side and gestured for Mary Ellis to come with her. Mary Ellis noticed for the first time, the keys that hung around her neck on a hot pink keychain. The woman walked around the edge of the library to its front door, not checking if Mary Ellis was coming with her. She jammed one of the keys into the keyhole of the door and jiggled it around for a moment before the door sprang open.

"You must really be in a rush to get something," the woman chimed, finally casting a glance over her shoulder. Mary Ellis just nodded, eager to get away from her. The woman didn't carry the same calming demeanor as Linda or David did, the whole town didn't. The woman laughed a tiny high pitched laugh and let Mary Ellis pass her.

"You go on, kid. See you around."

Mary Ellis immediately headed as far as she could from the woman, who was placing her things behind the front desk and logging into the large computer. She rushed away from the front desk towards the back of the library, where she hoped that the Yellow Pages would be kept. She poked around for a little while, walking between the shelves, scanning for the title of the book she needed, but it seemed as if this library didn't stock any Yellow Pages, at least not in the non-fiction Y section. As Mary Ellis was winding through the shelves for the third time, she glanced up to see a tall man striding towards her. Instinctively, she attempted to shrink back into the books that surrounded her, but it seemed the man was determined.

"Are you looking for something in particular?" the man asked, giving her a pained smile.

Mary Ellis stared blankly at him for a moment. Then she slowly took in his whole appearance, noticing the lanyard swinging from his neck with what seemed to be an identification badge hanging off of it. Suddenly realizing his purpose, Mary Ellis nodded slowly.

"Well, I can help you find anything you need." The man had a hand on his hip, in a way that conveyed an excess of energy rather than frustration, his feet bounced slightly.

"I was wondering if you all carried the Yellow Pages." Mary Ellis willed strength into her voice.

The man gave a nearly condescending laugh. "Not anymore, but I can show you how to access the White Pages on one of our computers. Is that alright?"

Mary Ellis just nodded.

"Alright, well let me just show you over here." He began to walk briskly towards one of the computers that lined the back wall of the library. Taking in a short breath, Mary Ellis followed closely behind the young librarian.

Almost moving mechanically, the man logged onto a computer and pulled up the White Pages website. Pointing to the search bar at the top of the screen he said, "Here you input the name of the person you want to find or an address."

Mary Ellis frowned; the way the man spoke was slow and drawn out, incredibly patronizing. She forced out a "thank you," hoping the man would disappear as quickly as possible. As soon as the man was gone she selected one of her parents at random, typing "Rachel Walker" into the search bar and waiting for a moment. The computer seemed to be sluggish in its motions as well, working its hardest to ensure that Mary Ellis didn't reach her goal.

Eventually the page loaded, and Mary Ellis scanned the list of names looking for her mother. Of the Rachel Walkers that were currently living in North Carolina, and there did seem to be a few, only one had a past address listed as "23 N. Fisher St. Apartment 2D Pineville, NC 28134." Though the apartment number wasn't listed, Mary Ellis figured she could make some assumptions. She clicked on the response that she believed was her mother and a full report appeared on the screen. Four previous addresses appeared on the screen, the most recent was still in North Carolina. Mary Ellis took a piece of paper from the bin next to the computers and scribbled down the most recent address. Nervous that it may be incorrect, she neatly recorded all of the other addresses as well as all previous phone numbers. Stuffing the piece of paper back into her pocket, Mary Ellis regarded the rest of the information on the screen.

Scrolling to the bottom of the page, Mary Ellis was met with a list of related persons. Joyce M. Walker was the first person on the list. Gran. Next to her name there was no marker indicating that she was dead or deceased, as Mary Ellis guessed she would be listed on a professional website such as this. It was strange to see her alive, at least in some ways, on the White Pages, her current address still listed as Mary Ellis's past home in Parkville. Mary Ellis guessed she could still be there, lying face up in the center of her bed. Rotting. Alone. Mary Ellis shuddered, clicking off of the page and back to her mother's.

Now she selected her father's (David E. Summers) name from the related person's list. She scanned the sparse information on his page. Phone numbers, aliases (Johnathan Weiss, David Walker, Matthew DeBois, "that's strange" Mary Ellis would think later, but at the moment she was too consumed with the search,) then addresses. The current address listed for her father was not the same as her mother's current address. This thought stopped her in her tracks. Removing her hands from her keyboard, Mary Ellis sat back in her chair. If this was true, and it may not be, Gran had always been sure to remind Mary Ellis never to trust what she read online, but if it were true then something had happened. Divorce or merely separation, either way her parents were not together. Or the website was wrong. It had to be wrong

Mary Ellis felt like the world was crumbling around her. This wasn't the way it was supposed to be. She knew that things would have probably changed since she last saw her parents, but they were supposed to still be together. They were supposed to be there for her. What would happen now that she could only live with her mother? Would it be like it was with Gran? No, it couldn't be. Her mother had to be kind.

Then why did she leave Mary Ellis. Mary Ellis's knuckles were white as she gripped the edge of the desk. So long she had been moving forward, towards her parents, in such a blind state. She had to believe that her parents were waiting for her because what else was there to do? It was this or let social services take her. It had seemed so clear in her bedroom at Gran's; the journey seemed so new, but now it just seemed useless. Her parents weren't together, they were probably liars, they'd probably forgotten about her by now.

Mary Ellis felt frozen, truly unsure of herself for the first time since she left. Though she'd been nervous before this moment, she'd always had a direction, something to be striving towards. Now, Mary Ellis didn't know what to do. Should she head home? Admit that this was useless and beg to be put in a home close to Parkville, close to Stacy?

No. She had to continue on, at least until she was sure that her parents didn't want her. There was no place to go but forward.

Shaking, Mary Ellis removed the piece of paper from her pocket and scribbled down the final addresses for her father. Without thinking, she exited out of the website and sat in front of the blank screen.

After a moment, Mary Ellis stood up from the table and glanced around the library. She watched for a moment as other patrons walked around the library in relative silence. They all seemed at least a little serene, unaffected by what Mary Ellis had just realized. None even glanced up to acknowledge that someone had moved in their presence. Realizing that no one was going to look at her, Mary Ellis exited the library, feeling that she should have been relieved. She was inconspicuous, no one even noticing what she was up to, that she was going to have to travel a little farther by herself.

Mary Ellis was alone.

She left the library without another thought, feeling empty. Once she was outside, she reached for the list of addresses in her pocket, once more assuring that they were still there, and stepped out into the street. What else could she do?

Chapter Eighteen

A little while after she had started through town, Mary Ellis stole a map from a hotel lobby, retreating before anyone noticed the small girl standing by the counter. Now, she traced her path, searching only for the town where her mother seemed to live, not yet able to find the exact address. All the energy felt sapped from her, and that made it feel strange to Mary Ellis that only a day ago she was filled with excitement and anxiety. Now she felt little, merely focusing on her work, the path that awaited her.

She would be spending a long time walking along the edge of the highway, ensuring that she kept sunscreen slathered all over her body to avoid the blistering sunburn she knew was possible. Shortly after she began her walk, Mary Ellis ran out of water and only a little after that her throat began to burn.

"This sucks," she mumbled. No one replied.

In her head though, Mary Ellis heard her grandmother.

"Nothing you've ever experienced is truly terrible," she'd say, "I'm giving you a good life."

In the past, Mary Ellis would have argued with her then. If the conversation was about something minor, Mary Ellis would list all the stupid gripes she had about her teachers or her home or the things that she had and Gran would tut at her, leaving Mary Ellis to stew over whatever frustrated her. If they were locked in a screaming match though, if Gran had grabbed her arms too roughly or forgot her birthday or called her particularly bad names, Mary Ellis would scream about the things she truly cared about: her mother and father, the way Gran always talked down to her and forced her to live without, isolated from everyone else in her grade.

This was when Gran would say the worst things, call her worthless and hideous. Call her a bastard. Now though, Mary Ellis knew Gran was right to say that. Her life was good. A bed and food and friendship seemed to be all that she could ever ask for.

She walked as far as she could that day following the map until it was too dark for her to read it. When finished, she slipped off the edge of the road, hunkering down in a rut just off the edge of the highway. Lying flat on her back, Mary Ellis watched the sky above her. It was a clear night and the stars shone brighter than they ever had in the town where she grew up. The sky was so vast and beneath them, Mary Ellis realized something. The world was so wide that if she were to disappear, no one would know where she went. Even if someone was to find her she was so far from home that they couldn't know who she was. Truly, if she became lost or forgot her parents and began to live on her own or if something were to happen to her, the world would move on. Things would continue to shift and change and Mary Ellis wouldn't have to deal with the consequences of any of it. She could go wherever people go, relying only on herself and casting everyone out.

But that could never be. Mary Ellis would never be satisfied if she didn't at least try to see if her parents would take her. Even if it was useless. Even if they never even cared about her. She had to at least complete her journey, feel its finality. Then she could figure out where to go from there.

Mary Ellis pressed her eyes shut, wishing that sleep would come quickly to her. It evaded her, though. Her mind raced with all that had happened that day.

It had been a long time since her mother lived at the address on the letters sent to her each year and her father could be gone. Something had happened, something was wrong. Mary Ellis needed to know what.

First, though, she needed to sleep. Eventually, she did: fitfully, full of dreams of futures too awful to describe, so that by the time she woke up, Mary Ellis was all too excited to start on her path again.

***

She assumed that at some point in the day she would get used to the sun beating on her head, but the sweat dripping like water down her face was a continuous reminder of heat. The sweat ran down her back, too, and even if the sweat were to subside, the burn in her throat caused by the lack of water was another constant reminder.

Mary Ellis wanted to sink down onto the ground and rest further, but she needed to press on. Thoughts ran through her mind: she should have refilled her water, she should have spent all the money she had left taking the bus again, but she just kept plodding on. There was nothing she could do now.

Sometime in the afternoon, after Mary Ellis's stomach had begun aching because she realized she had skipped breakfast and then lunch, too ready to continue on, a car pulled up beside Mary Ellis. A woman rolled down the window. She stared for a moment at Mary Ellis, who felt as if her legs were sagging under the weight of her body.

The woman had cherry red lips which smacked as she spoke. Her hand dangled out the window, as if it was reaching for Mary Ellis. Mary Ellis stared at her wrist, which was stacked with bangles.

"Hey, hon," she said brightly, sticking her face out of the window.

Behind her, Mary Ellis could see a skinny man with long, wiry hair who was tightly clutching the steering wheel. "What're you up to?" Mary Ellis could see a cigarette hanging from her messily painted fingers, smoking slightly.

"I'm just walking." Mary Ellis could feel herself backing away from the woman, her brightness was overwhelming, almost intimidating.

"Where 'ya heading?"

Mary Ellis could imagine the woman as a cheerleader, smacking gum in her mouth, if she brushed her hair and put on tighter clothing.

"I'm just walking home," Mary Ellis said flatly.

"Well, you're a long way from home, honey. You're a long way from anywhere, at least if you're going in this direction."

Mary Ellis could hear a laugh in her voice.

"I promise I'm fine."

The girl laughed out loud.

"Come on, let me take a look at that map." She reached her other hand out of the window, grasping for it. "My name's Violet, let me take a look at it. Come on."

Reluctantly, Mary Ellis passed the map to Violet, who studied it for a moment.

"You're heading through Greenspring?" she asked, though they both knew the answer. Violet beamed. "We're going right through there. You need a ride?"

Mary Ellis adjusted her bags on her wrists, bringing new attention to the sweat dripping down her back. A ride would be helpful, possibly cutting the length of her trip by days, but there was something about the way that Violet smiled and the man next to her sulked without saying a word that put Mary Ellis off.

"Come on, we won't bite."

Violet let the cigarette drop to the ground, Mary Ellis watched it burn for a moment then stamped it out with her foot. She took a shaky breath. With Violet in the car, the man couldn't do anything to her.

"Okay." Mary Ellis felt her voice was on the edge of breaking.

"You're too cute. Get in."

Mary Ellis flung the door open and threw her backpack inside of the back seat and climbed in after it. The air smelled like stale cigarettes and it was littered with food wrappers and beer bottles. There was shattered glass under one of the seats.

"This is Dylan." Violet poked a thumb at the man slouched in the seat next to her. He looked up into the rearview mirror at Mary Ellis, raising her eyebrows in greeting. Mary Ellis gave him a tight lipped smile.

"Hi," Mary Ellis murmured.

"He's a little bit moody, but nice deep down." Violet elbowed him slightly swerving the car just a little bit. Dylan smiled slightly. "What's your name, hon?"

"Mary Ellis."

"Where you coming from? You don't seem like a Carolina girl."

For a moment, Mary Ellis wanted to let the truth flow out of her. To tell the whole story to someone who wouldn't care about the fact that she was on the run. Violet and Dylan seemed effortless. Violet's ill-fitting clothes hung off her skinny frame, her hair clasped back to keep it from hanging in her face, perfectly framing her tiny features. Dylan's tight fitting shirt bore the logo of a band that Mary Ellis had never heard of. She needed to ensure her safety, though, and she was so close to making it to her parents, so close.

"Actually, I'm from North Carolina," Mary Ellis spat out instead, "but my parents and I moved up to Pennsylvania a couple of years ago. I'm just trying to come see my grandmother, because she is sick."

"Alone? Walking along the side of the road?" Violet squinted at her through the rearview mirror, when she locked eyes with Mary Ellis, she smiled.

"Yep." Mary Ellis nodded.

"Alright, you don't need to tell me what you're really up to but you shouldn't just lie about it."

"Sorry."

Mary Ellis tucked her feet up under herself, in order to avoid stepping on the broken glass.

"Dylan and I are taking a little vacation down the coast."

"She says that we are cementing our love for each other," Dylan finally said, bringing even more joy to Violet's face. Violet laughed and punched him in the arm again, harder.

"You make me sound cheesy. We're just road tripping," Violet said, her voice trailing off towards then end of the sentence. She blushed. Mary Ellis didn't care, she just sunk back into the seat and tried to enjoy herself while Violet and Dylan chattered to themselves, silently praying that they'd stop somewhere where she could get a drink. They quickly became background noise.

Mary Ellis watched through the window as a desolate industrial landscape sped by. Squat concrete buildings lined the road, between long stretches of commercial parks, grass just poking up between the cracks in the pavement. It wasn't the North Carolina she remembered the beaches that stretched as far as the eye could see and the warm, buzzing air.

"Hey, kid, can I see that map again?" Violet's hand poked into the back seat and waved around a bit, waiting. Wordless, Mary Ellis placed the map into Violet's hand, who spread it across the car's dashboard. As she focused on the route that was traced along it, Dylan snatched the map from her spreading it across the steering wheel.

"What are you doing? Let me handle it, V."

"I just want to see how far we can take her."

"I thought you said Greenspring?"

"We can go a little bit farther for this poor kid. We don't want her to bake in the heat, walking like she's trying to do."

Violet shot Dylan a goofy smile, but his mouth turned down into a frown. Mary Ellis studied her face in the mirror for a moment, she was younger than Mary Ellis originally thought. Mary Ellis would have originally said early twenties, but now teens seemed more apt. Mary Ellis could see the age on Dylan's face though, the wrinkles that creased his forehead and the corners of his eyes.

"I guess," he said, his displeasure poorly concealed, "Anyways, you can look at the map when we stop for dinner."

Violet giggled.

"Dinner?" Mary Ellis asked.

Dylan nodded.

"We'll go for a couple more hours then stop for the night."

"Okay." Mary Ellis's voice was quiet. The thought of spending so much time with these people made her stomach turn. Violet's sickly sweetness couldn't compensate for the aloofness of Dylan. Violet's voice was too loud, too bright. She was hiding just like Mary Ellis, maybe more so.

***

A couple of hours later, they pulled into a small diner on the side of the road. Violet bounced out of the car and Dylan followed her. They didn't check to see if Mary Ellis was following behind.

By the time Mary Ellis entered the diner, Dylan was just finishing talking to the waitress who was guiding them to their table. Mary Ellis scampered after them, settling next to Violet in the booth where they were seated. Violet seemed to be pouting slightly, her bottom lip stuck out like that of a cartoon child.

"I'm sure they wouldn't realize," Violet was hissing, but Dylan waved her off.

"You can never be too careful, V," Dylan said easily.

As Mary Ellis settled down, Dylan turned to look at her. Violet studied the menu in detail, occasionally reading off an option.

"When we're finished eating we're going to head to a motel, Violet and I have the room so you don't need to worry."

Mary Ellis just nodded, her head was buzzing with anxiety and a compulsion to get up and flee, but she stayed glued to her seat. Until they did something that was specifically bad, something that could harm her, Mary Ellis couldn't afford to waste the opportunity to get as close as she could to her parent's home.

"I think I'm going to have the chocolate chip pancakes. How about you, Mary?" Violet interjected.

"It's Mary Ellis, actually."

"Doesn't matter, what're you having?"

The sleeve of her thin sweater slipped over her shoulder, revealing the top of a pale pink bra, Violet didn't move to cover it. Instead she leaned down over the table,

162

letting it slide further down her chest. Mary Ellis could barely tear her eyes from Violet to look at the menu.

"I'll probably just have a grilled cheese sandwich." Mary Ellis tried to focus on the menu, not looking up. Violet laughed.

A waiter appeared at the table and took their drink orders. Violet giggled to the waiter, attracting Dylan's glare. As the waiter walked away, Dylan grabbed the sleeve of Violet's sweater and tugged it back over her shoulder. Violet frowned at him.

"Tell us about yourself," Dylan started, but Violet waved her off.

"The kid doesn't want to talk about herself, she made that very clear in the car."

Dylan grunted.

"Not that you were paying attention."

Mary Ellis could feel tension beginning to pool in the small booth. She began to feel hyper aware of the places where she and Violet's bodies touched: gently at the knee, just slightly on the upper arms near the shoulder.

The waiter came again with a tray of drinks and set them down at each person's place.

"What will you be having to eat?" the waiter asked, "Or do you need any more time to think about it."

"We're fine. She'll have the chocolate chip pancakes with syrup on the side, she'll have a grilled cheese, and I'll have." Dylan considered the menu for a moment, his hair tickling the edge of the menu. "A vegetable omelet."

"Great we should have that out to you shortly."

Dylan shot the waiter a wide smile, his canines were so sharp they looked like fangs.

The waiter walked quickly away and Dylan turned back to Mary Ellis.

"You shouldn't be afraid of us. We have just as much to lose from being found out as you do." His voice was a low grumble that Mary Ellis felt was meant for only her to hear. It rang around in her head.

"I just-"

"I know I don't understand exactly what you're going through, but I do understand the importance of playing your cards close to your chest. We're helping you out, you know you can trust us."

"I don't think it's a good idea to tell you," Mary Ellis said.

Violet finally turned her attention back to Mary Ellis. "Come on. Don't be boring."

"I just don't want to put myself at risk. I don't know you."

"What did you do? You're too young to have killed anyone and I can't imagine anyone is coming after you so what are you so afraid of. What could we do?" Violet braced her hands on the edge of the table. Mary Ellis sighed as she watched Violet's eyes; they were too eager.

"Call the police," Mary Ellis mumbled, anger beginning to burn inside her, "or send me back home." Immediately after the words left her mouth, Mary Ellis wish she hadn't said it. Violet's eyes bulged, taking in the secret.

"I knew you were a runaway," Violet almost squealed. "What are you on the run from, Mary?" Her tone was almost sing song-y.

Mary Ellis was silent.

Dylan leaned back in his seat, looking Mary Ellis up and down.

"I'll tell you more about me," Violet said then she lowered her voice slightly, leaning forward, "I'm a runaway, too."

Mary Ellis nodded blankly.

164

"And Dylan?" Mary Ellis trailed off.

"Well Dylan, he's..." The conversation lapsed into silence and Mary Ellis watched as Dylan scanned the restaurant, possibly looking for their waiter.

It just so happened that the waiter was walking towards their table, holding a tray of food above his head. He stopped at their table, placing a plate in front of each of the customers sitting at the table.

"Let me know if you need anything else," he said, before speeding back off towards the kitchen.

Silence settled in over the table as Violet began to dig into her food. Mary Ellis took a few small bites, but Dylan just sat on the other side of the table, staring at the girls on the other side of him.

Mary Ellis finished her food as quickly as possible and watched as Violet and Dylan finished eating and paid the check. For a moment, Mary Ellis thought she should offer to pay for their dinner, but then confidence filled her and she realized that she deserved it. She deserved having someone spend the money on her, she deserved the food.

They walked out into the parking lot and clambered into the car. A relative silence still settled over the group, allowing Mary Ellis to fade into drowsiness in the back seat of the car. She heard Dylan and Violet sharing words on occasion, but Mary Ellis wasn't listening. Even when they pulled into a tiny motel, Mary Ellis let herself be almost pulled through the parking lot and into the lobby. She didn't pay attention as Dylan bought a room with two double beds and Violet took her hand and dragged her up the steps and then they were in the room. Violet was slipping off her sweatpants and climbing into bed, while Dylan was changing into pajama bottoms he had gotten from their large suitcase and coming into her bed right after her. Mary Ellis tried to avoid watching them as they cuddled together under the covers.

"Can you get the light when you're ready for bed?" Violet asked, already ignoring the young girl before the question even exited her mouth.

"Sure," Mary Ellis said, crossing the room and sending it all into darkness then quickly scampering back to the other bed in the room.

"Goodnight," Violet's voice chimed from across the room, the giggle returning to her voice as she nestled closer to Dylan.

Mary Ellis didn't reply. Instead, she just climbed into her bed and pulled the blankets over her. The anxiety leapt up in her again as the room went almost silent. In the darkness, anything could happen. Dylan and Violet could hurt or abandon her. Occasionally, she would hear a tiny sound come from the bed next to her, but otherwise the room remained trapped in silence.

Chapter Nineteen

Mary Ellis awoke to Violet pushing at her side. She was standing on the side of the bed, her large eyes blinking down at Mary Ellis. She was already dressed in a different set of baggy, ill-fitting clothes and had a dusting of makeup settled on her face.

"Wake up, honey," Violet said. "It's time to get going."

Mary Ellis shook the grogginess from her body as she sat up. Violet was clearly a morning person.

"Do you need to borrow some clothes? I looked through your bag and it didn't look like you had much."

Mary Ellis's eyes widened, there had to be something wrong with her.

"Don't worry I put everything back."

"I guess that would be nice. Thanks," Mary Ellis mumbled, climbing out of bed. She glanced around the room, light was pouring in through the curtains that Violet had flung open. Dylan was slipping a shirt over his head as Mary Ellis turned around to face them and Violet had crossed the room and was pulling an outfit out of her bag.

"Morning," Dylan muttered.

Mary Ellis just nodded at him as Violet threw a bundle of clothing at her.

"Do you think I have time to shower?" Mary Ellis asked.

Violet laughed. "Of course you do."

Mary Ellis quickly crossed the room and entered into the motel's tiny bathroom. Last night she had even been too tired to brush her teeth, but now Mary Ellis was eager to wash with hot water once again. As she stepped into the shower, Mary Ellis caught a glimpse of her reflection. Suddenly she was glad that she had enough time to shower before she saw her mother. Her hair was a rat's nest and her face was what could best be described as grimy. Mary Ellis looked away from the mirror and climbed into the shower, pulling the curtain so she couldn't see the light or the mirror through the gap. Mary Ellis quickly washed herself and climbed out.

The room was empty as Mary Ellis stepped out into it, so she pulled on the clothes that were sitting in a pile on the edge of her bed, they hung off her small frame, but Mary Ellis didn't care.

"Violet?" Mary Ellis asked, but the air in the room was still. She peeked out into the hallway, looking at the doors up and down the hall, but it was empty as well. She'd wait a little while, and get on the road if they didn't come back soon.

For twenty minutes, Mary Ellis sat frozen on the edge of her bed. She barely glanced around the room, just praying that Violet and Dylan would be back soon. Anxiety had burrowed into her chest.

After five more minutes, Mary Ellis realized she'd need to leave. There was no point waiting around here if they weren't coming back, so she picked up her backpack and left the room, hoping that she could find Violet and Dylan before they left without her, leaving her in a town she didn't recognize.

Mary Ellis walked into the hallway and quickly started down to the lobby where she hoped Violet and Dylan would be waiting for her. As she entered the lobby, Mary Ellis's breath hitched. There was no one there. The anxiety in Mary Ellis's heart began to rise as she sped out into the parking lot. The car that Violet and Dylan used was missing. Mary Ellis could feel her heart pounding in her chest.

Eyes burning, Mary Ellis went back into the motel and walked up to her room, dizzy and unsure of what to do. Violet hadn't given back the map that she had taken from Mary Ellis the day prior and without it, Mary Ellis needed a new one. She'd need to get a map from the lobby and try to retrace all the parts of the directions that she remembered. Then, she could continue on without having to worry about Violet and Dylan any more. It would take much longer and Mary Ellis may have to pay more, but at least then Mary Ellis could get moving without concern.

Entering the lobby for the second time that morning, still with no sign of where Violet and Dylan had run off to, Mary Ellis was overcome with a new sense of serenity. She approached the receptionist with what she hoped was a collected authority about her own situation, and for once this matched what she felt inside.

"Hey, honey, how can I help you?" The woman looked down absentmindedly at Mary Ellis.

"Do you have a map that I could use?" Mary Ellis asked, fishing around in one of her bags for the list of addresses. She smoothed it out on her thigh then shoved it back in her pocket. As she waited for the receptionist's reply, Mary Ellis grabbed a pen from the cap that sat on the edge of the counter.

As the woman had been silent for a long moment and Mary Ellis was finished working, Mary Ellis looked up at her.

Her brow was furrowed and there were a bit of discomfort and maybe pity in her eyes.

"Ma'am?" Mary Ellis asked.

The woman's eyes widened in surprise, as if she had forgotten Mary Ellis existed.

"Why doesn't your father come down here and get it for you?"

"My father?" Mary Ellis asked, but immediately wanted to stuff the words back into her mouth. Dylan. "Yeah sorry, he asked me to get them for him."

The creases in the receptionist's forehead became deeper.

"Okay," she said eventually, looking too concerned, "I'm going to give you one but you need to promise not to do anything bad. You need to promise to give it to your daddy and not run off with it."

Cheeks burning, Mary Ellis muttered, "promise," and marched out of the motel. That was it. She would just have to start out on her own with no direction. Scowling, Mary Ellis turned and sped through the parking lot.

Heat crackled through the air as Mary Ellis crossed through the parking lot and started down the road. Almost immediately she began to regret wearing Violet's pants as the material itched and clung to her body, trapping the heat to her legs. At first, each time a car passed Mary Ellis's head would snap up and scan the horizon for Violet and Dylan, but after about twenty minutes the sounds faded into the background.

Mary Ellis's head hung as she continued along the highway. She wasn't sure how long it had been, but she hadn't seen a single building on the side of the road, only long stretches of short grass interspersed with the occasional tree. Suddenly, Mary Ellis felt a car pull up next to her and ease to a stop. Heart suddenly seizing, Mary Ellis continued at a faster pace, not looking up at what she assumed was a potential captor. Then she heard it.

"Hey, dummy, what are you doing?" Mary Ellis heard a familiar voice laugh from the car. Her shoulders relaxed.

"Sorry," Mary Ellis mumbled, turning towards the car.

Violet sat in the passenger's seat and was leaning out the window towards Mary Ellis, Dylan was in the driver's seat.

"Well, get in."

Violet slid back into the car and twisted around, flinging open Mary Ellis's door. Mary Ellis scampered into the car and shut the door behind her. Violet was watching her through the rearview mirror. As Mary Ellis met her eyes, she smiled.

"Where did you go?" Mary Ellis asked, "Why did you leave me? I was just taking a shower and you left without me."

"We were going to get breakfast," Dylan scoffed, "no need to be so obnoxious about it."

"Yeah, I left a note." Violet grinned and passed a crumpled paper bag to Mary Ellis. "We got this for you, not sure what you liked."

"I didn't see it." Mary Ellis peeled open the bag to reveal a small egg sandwich, she pulled it out.

"Well, whose fault is that?"

"Dylan," Violet chided, giving him a light punch on the arm. "Why didn't you wait for us? We would have come back."

"I'm used to being left."

Mary Ellis watched as Violet folded her own legs up onto the seat and dove into her own paper bag. She sighed as Mary Ellis spoke.

"Well, we're here now and we have you. Everything's all right."

"Thanks," Mary Ellis said meekly, polishing off the last of the egg sandwich. "Do you have my map?"

"Yeah, hon."

"Can I see it?" Violet twisted around in her seat and passed the map to Mary Ellis, who spread it over her lap.

"Where were you going to leave me again?"

"Greenspring," Dylan said, his eyes focused on the road. Mary Ellis nodded and began to fold up the map for a moment, then stopped. She searched for a street sign or some other sign of where they were. After a few minutes she spotted a rusted street sign on the side of the highway and traced her place on the map. They were close.

After about an hour of Mary Ellis staring out the window, legs bouncing in anticipation of the progress she'd made, the car passed a 'Welcome to Greenspring' sign. Mary Ellis shook herself out of the haze of car travel and sat up.

"Where are you going to let me out?"

"Not sure, we'll know it when we see it," Dylan said, and Mary Ellis felt her pulse beginning to race. She squinted slightly at Dylan, who wasn't watching her. They continued on without another thought.

As they continued through the streets of Greenspring, eventually the houses which lined the road began to thin out, until they were continuing along the same almost desolate landscape they had been on for the two days prior. When Mary Ellis was sure they had left Greenspring, the fear in her began to rise.

"Dylan," she whispered, "where are we going?"

Finally, he looked back at her in the mirror, then made eye contact with Violet, who was looking slightly concerned. "We're going to go out of the way and take you a little bit farther."

"Okay." Mary Ellis's heart began to leap in her chest.

"I felt bad letting a young girl like you walk all alone." Dylan's voice had grown colder. At first she hadn't noticed the change, but now it was there plain as day. Mary Ellis looked to Violet, attempting to make contact with the one comfort she had in the car. Violet had opened the glove box and was staring inside, unmoving. Growing frantic for a warmth on which to hold, Mary Ellis turned back to the map. She pulled the map back over her lap and stared down at it, trying to orient herself to their location. Staring at the street signs and town markings she slowly traced her way to where they were. They were going in the wrong direction. Her heartbeat rose into her throat and her head was swimming. Her mouth flopped open for a moment, before she spoke.

"We're going the wrong way," Mary Ellis said, more meekly then she intended. She saw Violet's eyes flare, but Dylan retained his calm demeanor.

"I'm taking a different route."

Mary Ellis's breath began to hitch and her throat felt bone dry.

"When are you dropping me off?"

"Tomorrow morning. We're going to stay the night in another motel."

Mary Ellis folded the map up and placed it in her bag, trying to steady her breathing. She pulled the backpack up into her lap and wanted to bury her face into it, but she just stared out the window instead. The squat buildings and cars flew past her even faster.

When they eased into the parking lot of the motel later that day, after a tense and quiet dinner, Mary Ellis was still buzzing with anxiety, wracking her brain for a way to escape the couple. Violet climbed out of the car, opening the door for Mary Ellis, while Dylan just swept past the two girls into the motel's lobby. Mary Ellis watched Violet as they crossed the parking lot. Something had went missing in her too. No longer was she the peppy and excitable girl she had been in days prior, now she seemed slightly empty, her eyes staring vacantly at the pavement. She didn't say a word. When they entered the lobby, Dylan immediately ushered them back outside once again, having already purchased their room for the night. They walked up a flight of stairs and along a concrete path overlooking the parking lot and surrounding highway. The sun was setting on the horizon, blazing the skyline with oranges and pinks. Mary Ellis watched the sun as Dylan unlocked their door. When the door was open, Violet grabbed her hand and pulled her into their room. As the door shut behind Mary Ellis, she felt like it was the last time she was ever going to see the sun.

This room was smaller, the beds so close together Mary Ellis could lie on one and reach out and touch the other, and the whole place smelled of must. There was a tiny TV perched on a dresser in front of the two beds and a small end table between them, but nothing else in the way of furniture. Thick deep red curtains were pulled tight over a window that overlooked the parking lot, leaving the room in a deep haze even when Dylan flicked on the tiny lamp that sat on the end table and the faint overhead light.

Immediately, Violet bolted towards the bathroom.

"I'm going to shower," she called, the door already shut behind her. Suddenly, the room seemed incredibly cramped and Mary Ellis felt incredibly alone. Dylan was standing beside one of the beds peeling off his T-shirt and jeans. Then he was standing in his underwear. Then he was lying in one of the beds and turning on the TV and looking at Mary Ellis and asking her:

"What are you doing just standing there?"

And Mary Ellis stumbled over her words as she struggled to reply, "Nothing. Just looking around. Sorry."

Dylan scoffed and eased back into the bed, turning his gaze back to the TV. When Mary Ellis heard the shower start, she jolted. She crossed the room in a daze and climbed into the other bed, placing her backpack under the covers next to her. She pulled the blanket high around her neck.

"Aren't you going to put on pajamas? You've been in those clothes all day," Dylan said, keeping his eyes locked on the TV.

"I don't have any."

"Well, Violet needs those back, so why don't you change into some of your other clothes?"

Mary Ellis's skin crawled.

"I'll just change tomorrow morning."

"I want to go and wash them tonight."

Mary Ellis sighed, her lungs feeling caught in her throat, but she nodded at Dylan.

"I'll wait for Violet to get out then."

"She's going to be a long while." Dylan picked up the remote from the bed and changed the channel. The nighttime news blared from the TV's tiny speakers, something about a children's toy being recalled because it caused them to choke.

"Okay," Mary Ellis said, and took in a shaky breath. She stood up from the bed, standing as far as she could from Dylan, and took her bag from under the covers. She peeled open the bag and took a T-shirt and shorts from inside, turned to face the wall, and pulled Violet's shirt off her head, replacing it with her own T-shirt as quickly as she could. Mary Ellis could feel Dylan's eyes raking her back and almost shivered, but kept her composure. She shimmied her pants off and slipped the new shorts on. Then she dove onto the bed, keeping herself as far as she could from him. When she turned over to face the rest of the room, Dylan was watching the TV intently once again.

Mary Ellis heard the shower turn off and shuddered. A long while. She tucked herself into the bed as best she could and tried to settle down.

After a moment, Mary Ellis heard a whisper from the other bed, "You're a very pretty girl." It was so quiet that at first Mary Ellis wasn't even sure that it had been said, but when she peeked up from underneath the nest of blankets that she had created for herself, she saw Dylan's face, wide as a moon, grinning at her. The first time she had seen him really smile in their time knowing each other. Once again his eyes were cold.

Then the thin door to the bathroom flapped open and Violet walked out into the center of the room in a new set of pajamas. She didn't seem to be totally herself again, but she was smiling. She turned off the faint overhead light as she walked by it, then the light on the end table. Then she climbed into bed next to Dylan. Mary Ellis could just barely see Violet snuggle up to him and she pressed her eyes shut, just trying to bide the time until they went to sleep.

For hours Dylan sat up in the bed just watching the TV, occasionally flipping the channel, with Violet curled at his side, sleeping soundly. Eventually, though, Dylan turned away from the TV and Mary Ellis heard the sound of his breathing slip into a rhythm. Still she waited for a little while. When she was almost positive that both Violet and Dylan were asleep, Mary Ellis swung her feet over the edge of the bed and stepped onto the floor. It seemed to creak so loudly under her feet, but she crept across the floor, her backpack slung over her back. As she passed by Violet and Dylan's bed, she almost held her breath, especially when Violet shifted in the bed and sat up, blinking her large eyes at Mary Ellis. Mary Ellis scrunched up her face and stopped, turning to face Violet.

"I'm leaving," Mary Ellis whispered. Violet was lit only by the faint blue light of the TV, she frowned. "Please don't tell Dylan. Please don't wake him up."

Violet paused. For a moment it seemed she was trying to unravel herself from Dylan's arms and rise up from the bed. She reached her arm out towards Mary Ellis and then dropped it. She nodded, seeming a bit frazzled and sighed before speaking.

"Okay," Violet said, and smiled slightly. Dylan stirred in her arms, but didn't wake up. "I hope you make it to wherever you are going."

"I hope you do, too," Mary Ellis said.

As Violet smiled, Dylan began to stir in her arm.

Taking a shaky breath, Violet pressed back into him, mumbling something into his ear, her face seeming to droop as she pressed back down into Dylan's arm. Mary Ellis passed by the bed to the door and then turned around, looking back at Violet, who was peeking over Dylan's shoulder. She smiled at the girl in the bed. Then she walked out the door. There were few cars in the parking lot as Mary Ellis walked out onto the concrete, but the moon had spread itself out over the North Carolina night. Mary Ellis looked up at it, smiling. She let herself lean out over the balcony and stare down at the scene below, smiling right back. Other than Dylan's small dark car in the corner of the lot, there was no sign of those who Mary Ellis feared would become her pursuers or worse, her captors.

Mary Ellis wanted to shiver; there were ripples of fear underneath her skin, but the night air was warm and swampy and hugged Mary Ellis, keeping her warm. She felt safe. Then she remembered where she was and pulled the map out of her pocket and started down the walkway towards the stairs. She stepped out of the stairwell and felt free of everything. She wanted to run across the parking lot and back down the highway and straight into her mother's arms, but she needed to conserve her energy. Mary Ellis already felt tired and heavy, but needed to make it as far as she could before the night was over.

Mary Ellis had decided that it would be better to travel during the night from then on. She wasn't sure if Dylan would come looking for her, but she wasn't going to let him find her.

Mary Ellis walked out of the parking lot and started down the highway in the direction she had come that afternoon. Occasionally, a car would speed past her and if she couldn't see it at first, Mary Ellis's heart would leap in fear, only settling when she could see that the car wasn't Dylan's. Still, she plodded along. When her whole body was sagging and anxiety had exhausted her, Mary Ellis pressed on, only stopping when the sun reached the horizon. Then she stumbled off the side of the road until she was just far enough that she wouldn't be seen, collapsed onto the ground, and fell into a deep, exhausted sleep.

Chapter Twenty

It was dusk when Mary Ellis awoke once again, and rain had begun to fall in droves. Already, she was soaked to the bone and cold, her T-shirt and shorts clinging to her body. She sat up and glanced around for a moment. Cars cluttered the highway, loud enough that Mary Ellis was surprised they hadn't woken her up. She shifted her focus to her bags which were, much to Mary Ellis's dismay, lying splayed open next to her. The rain had come and had soaked through everything she had, all of her other clothes and the books, which were now less than useless, and, upon further inspection, most of her food as well. The only things that were left untouched were the cans of beans that Mary Ellis had disregarded until this moment, there had always been something else that would have been easier to prepare, and a now nearly empty loaf of bread, protected only by a thin layer of plastic.

Mary Ellis pried open the loaf of bread, her fingers aching with cold, and took out the last two slices. She scarfed them down with little regard for who could see, and threw the plastic bag on the ground with the rest of her things.

Now, Mary Ellis would have to hold off eating as long as possible, hoping that she could find somewhere else to get food before the urge to eat became stronger than her will. She didn't even have utensils or a way to produce a fire that could heat the beans. She hoped more than anything that she wouldn't have to resort to cold beans.

Finally, Mary Ellis began to pick through all of her things, thinking that she could condense her belongings into one bag. As she began to remove all of her clothing from the bag where she kept them, the photograph of her Gran, Grandpa and mother fluttered to the ground. Mary Ellis stared down at it; the faces were warped by the onslaught of water, all of the figures, but especially her mother, were bloated by the water damage. Mary Ellis would never be able to recognize them. After a moment, she turned from the picture and continued to transfer her clothes from one bag to another.

She finished after a couple of minutes, shoving the second plastic bag, no longer needed, into the bulging first. Finally, she checked her pockets to ensure there wasn't a morsel of food she could be forgetting.

In the front left pocket of her jean shorts, her parent's letter was tucked away. Using a wet sweatshirt as a shield, Mary Ellis removed the letter from her pocket. It was damp, but she could still make out the message it once held. The address in the top left corner. It was salvageable. Mary Ellis stared down at it, her mother's loopy handwriting, similar to Gran's, but just different enough. Frustration began to swell in Mary Ellis, she was so close. She'd thought she was so close. Now though, freezing cold and soaking wet and with no idea how far she was from where she needed to go, Mary Ellis felt there was almost no point to going on. In an angry fit Mary Ellis crushed the letter in her fist and then released it, letting it flutter to the ground. She watched for a moment as the water began to pelt the letter's surface.

Almost without thought, Mary Ellis turned away from whatever couldn't be salvaged and started back towards the highway, hoping that somehow she could reach her mother's new address before night fell once again.

She started down the road once again, paying little mind to those who passed by her. At first she trudged in silence, staring at the ground and only moving her body forward. One foot in front of the other. Eventually, though, when she could no longer bear merely the sounds of the rain pelting down and cars rushing by, Mary Ellis began to speak.

"Stacy," she said quietly, at once able to taste the rain, "I think that maybe it would have been a good idea to have gotten help."

"From who? I'm not sure. David probably since he was so close." For a moment Mary Ellis was silent. She could imagine what Stacy would have said. The lilt of her quiet voice and the way it sometimes flew out of her, seemingly without Stacy's consent.

"Maybe I should have gone to the police." Another moment passed, Mary Ellis glanced around. She watched rain beat down on the trees, forming puddles on the ground. Her limbs felt heavy.

"Maybe I should have gone to the police in the first place."

A tractor trailer sped past, sending a spray of water over Mary Ellis's body. She shuddered.

"But I'm here now." Outside of her mind, Mary Ellis's voice sounded near vacant, defeated. She was just completing a task, accomplishing her goal. She just wanted it all to be finished. She wanted to be curled up in a warm bed, at this point she didn't care whose it was.

"I need help," Mary Ellis said. She realized that at this point she was yelling but for the moment she didn't care.

After her outburst, Mary Ellis kept her mouth locked shut. Talking to herself was one thing but screaming about needing help on the highway was another entirely. She'd need to be careful if she didn't want to attract attention. She'd need to conserve food if she wanted to eat. She'd need to conserve money for emergencies. She'd need to find some place to dry her clothes and herself if she wanted to keep warm.

It was all too much. The night dragged on.

***

The rain wasn't letting up, even as the sun breeched the horizon. Mary Ellis's clothes were plastered against her body, dragging her towards the earth. She was half tempted to try to settle down for the night, try to get some rest as her body was exhausted.

Still, she knew if she laid down now, sleep wouldn't come. Even if she could manage to find a place slightly sheltered from the droves of rain, there was no way she could completely avoid the rain. Besides, the road around was barren. She'd keep going until she found a place to stop. Mary Ellis couldn't afford to waste time.

"Stacy?" she asked, her mouth was instantly full of water. She coughed. Mary Ellis felt like she was drowning.

"I don't know what's happening anymore."

Mary Ellis craned her head towards the sky, expecting to see the stars sparkling above just as she had that night in the motel. The sky was blank, not even swirling with clouds, the air just hung static. A flat blanket.

"Please tell me what to do," she whispered.

There was no response.

Mary Ellis continued on until the rain felt like daggers on her skin. Until she was sure if she took another step the rain would plaster her to the pavement, but she continued on sure something had to come soon. There had to be somewhere she could settle down for the night.

After what felt like another hour, Mary Ellis felt like she needed to at least lie down. Weight dragged on her eyelids, pulling her towards the pavement. When she felt she couldn't continue on, Mary Ellis walked as far as she could off the road and hunkered down.

She laid for as long as she could, pressing her eyes shut and trying to clear her mind, but sleep didn't come. Still, Mary Ellis felt exhausted. She didn't want to stand up and get back on the road. Her stomach growled, Mary Ellis figured she could crack into a can of beans now, if just to give her some strength.

Mary Ellis fished around in her bags for a moment before withdrawing one of the cans of beans. She pried it open with her fingers and took a swig of the cold beans. The beans were immediately flooded with rainwater, but Mary Ellis took another swig, gagging as the bean water reached the back of her throat.

Slowly, she made her way back to the road, quietly eating beans as she went. Mary Ellis walked as the sun began to rise, but the rain showed no signs of ceasing. As the sun climbed higher and higher, Mary Ellis felt a chill reach deep into her bones. Though she had been shivering slightly for the whole night, now she was completely shaking. Hunger continued to ache in her stomach, but Mary Ellis stumbled on.

Mary Ellis wasn't sure how long it was until she spotted it. A green sign that looked tiny in the distance. Something was around. Mary Ellis cheered out loud. Her voice sounded hoarse. She wanted to run until she could see what the sign said, but she couldn't summon the strength. Instead, she just willed herself forward.

It took almost twenty minutes to reach the sign, which read "Rest Stop Ahead" with an arrow pointing to a road that shot off the highway. Mary Ellis started down the off ramp. It only took a short period until she arrived at the rest stop. All it was was a large parking lot for trailers and a small pavilion. It was empty.

Mary Ellis wandered to the pavilion and collapsed on the picnic table, enjoying the lack of rain pelting her. It was barely an instant before Mary Ellis fell into an exhausted sleep.

Chapter Twenty-One

When Mary Ellis woke, the moon was already making its way across the sky. She sat up, swearing under her breath as she realized what time it was. She hoisted herself off the ground, head pounding and back aching, a hunger growing in her stomach. Mary Ellis couldn't stop to eat, though. She had to make progress before the morning came, so she hiked back to the road and continued her journey forward. In a way, Mary Ellis felt fresh, clean, and new, but this just felt like work.

Then the rain continued. It soaked her quickly and kept coming, seeming to penetrate Mary Ellis down to the very bone. She wanted to wait at the pavilion set out all of her clothes so she could get dry, still, she had to continue. Mary Ellis pressed on through the night for almost an hour, until she began to shiver almost incessantly and she decided she would need to stop at the next place she saw. It had been a while since she saw anything other than swamplands and squat trees and bushes.

Mary Ellis didn't know what she would do to get to her mother's from wherever she found. If it was a motel she would consider staying, but that would leave her money supply severely lacking. If it was some type of store, well, Mary Ellis would just have to beg the employee on duty to let her stay for as long as she could. If wherever she stopped had a phone she would swallow her pride and just call someone. Then she wouldn't have to walk any longer and her feet wouldn't ache and she could sleep for a thousand hours and Mary Ellis and her parents would have grand meals around the dining room table. This brought a wide grin over Mary Ellis's face. Soon she would be with her family and she wouldn't have to fight any longer.

Still, Mary Ellis's hair clung to her face and a chill ran through her as she plodded down the side of the road. Sloshing through the growing puddles on the side of the highway, she considered dropping her bags and running as fast as she could, but then she remembered her clothes, and most importantly, money.

As she was beginning to think that hitchhiking may have been a good idea, Mary Ellis saw a glimmer of light on the horizon. The shining yellow and red sign of a Motel 6. Mary Ellis began to run down the road, rain wicking off her skin as she went. She reached the nearly deserted parking lot quickly and sped to the doorway. The doors flew open as she walked towards them and Mary Ellis passed through them. The lobby of the motel was bright and warm; a small cluster of chairs had been squeezed into one corner. Most of the lobby was taken up by the large front desk which was crowded with pamphlets for North Carolina attractions that Mary Ellis had never heard of before. Behind the desk, a tall woman with dusky eyeshadow swept about her eyes glared down at Mary Ellis, who was suddenly self-conscious about how much water she was dripping onto the floor.

"Welcome to Motel 6. What can I do to help you?" the woman, whose nametag said Bobby, said with a frown.

"Can I use your phone?"

Bobby looked Mary Ellis up and down.

"Please," Mary Ellis said, avoiding eye contact, "I just need to call a taxi."

Bobby's eyes softened slightly. "Sure, kid."

She picked up the phone, passing it across the desk to Mary Ellis.

"Do you know the number?"

Mary Ellis shook her head no and then watched as Bobby dialed it for her.

"Don't sit on any of the furniture," Bobby added as Mary Ellis walked away.

Mary Ellis nodded and took the phone, walking as far from the desk as its curly cord would let her. The phone operator for the taxi company answered and quickly arranged for a car to meet her there. When Mary Ellis hung up, she made eye contact with Bobby across the room, who beckoned her back towards the desk.

"Can I just call one more person?" Mary Ellis asked, trying her best to look cute so that Bobby would forget what she last said. "I just want to make sure my mom knows I'll be coming home in a taxi instead of walking."

Bobby sighed, and simply passed the phone back to Mary Ellis without another word. Before Mary Ellis dialed, Bobby had already returned to her computer screen her attention entirely diverted from Mary Ellis.

Quickly, Mary Ellis tapped Stacy's number into her phone.

It rang once. Twice. And then Mary Ellis heard her voice.

"Hello?"

Stacy's voice was groggy on the phone. Mary Ellis could hear her father yell something from another room. She realized that she wasn't sure how late it was.

"It's me," Mary Ellis said.

"Mary Ellis?"

"Yeah."

"Listen, I can't talk for long or my father'll wonder what's up."

Mary Ellis glanced around the room, in the corner; she spotted a clock. It was 11:30.

"Mary Ellis? Are you alright?" Stacy said.

Mary Ellis coiled the phone's cord between her fingers. She wasn't sure exactly what she wanted to say, but she knew it had to be something.

"I'm not sure what I'm doing. Where I should be going anymore."

"What? Mary Ellis," Stacy said, panic creeping into her voice, "What's wrong?"

Mary Ellis watched as the doors to the motel swung open and an old man entered. She watched as he approached the front desk and began to speak to Bobby.

"My parents weren't at the house where they'd been sending me letters from for all these years. The woman who answered the door said it had been years since they moved in." Mary Ellis felt tears prick the corners of her eyes. "I found another address for my mother but I don't know what I am going to do."

"Where are you now?"

"I'm at a Motel Six in North Carolina. I can't be any more specific. I'm getting a taxi. I can't walk anymore." Mary Ellis let out a sob. Bobby looked up from her computer, where she had begun to check the man into a room and made eye contact with her. Mary Ellis tried to smile at her.

"Do you need help? I can get my parents to-"

"No. I'll be okay, I'm just tired."

"Well, try to get some sleep. I miss you."

"How are-" Mary Ellis started, but another yell came from Stacy's side of the phone. Her father must be calling.

"I need to go, Mary Ellis. Please call me when you get there."

"Night."

Then the line went dead. Mary Ellis glanced around the lobby once again, Bobby was still watching her.

After a couple more minutes, Mary Ellis watched a car pull up in front of the motel, a taxi. Quickly, she thrust the phone at Bobby and rushed out the door. She clambered into the taxi, watching as the driver looked her up and down.

"Where ya' heading?" he asked, barely glancing at her once she was seated inside, her plastic bags piled around her.

Mary Ellis pulled the last of her money out of her pocket. "As far along this path that you can take me with this much money," Mary Ellis said, smoothing her map over her lap. She handed it to him, and he peered at it for a moment.

"How much do you have?" he asked, squinting at the map.

"Seven dollars."

The man leaned across Mary Ellis to open the passenger side door. He folded up her map, looking expectantly at her and then said, "I cannot take you that far with this little money. You must find some other way."

"Please, sir. Just take me as far as you can." Mary Ellis shoved the map into her bag and crushed the wad of money in her hand, shoving it into her pocket.

"I cannot leave you in the middle of nowhere. Get out. Please, ma'am." The man stared at her, pity in his eyes, but kept the door held open, waiting for her.

Mary Ellis kept still holding out hope for just a moment that he would give up and do what she wanted, but when he gestured once again towards the motel, Mary Ellis clambered out into the rain once again.

"I'm sorry," he said once more as he sped away.

Mary Ellis returned to the motel lobby, newly wet, newly cold. Besides Bobby the lobby was empty, and Mary Ellis sighed. There was no one to turn to now. No way forward that Mary Ellis could see clearly.

"What happened?" Bobby asked, not looking up at Mary Ellis.

"He wouldn't take me, said I didn't have enough money."

Bobby looked up. "How much do you have?"

Now it was Mary Ellis's turn to avoid her gaze. She stared at her own feet, which were shitting on the floor. "Seven dollars."

Bobby sighed. Mary Ellis watched as she exited out of her tab on the computer and then shut it down, making slow, deliberate movements. When the screen went black, Bobby stood up and walked around the counter, coming to rest in one of the chairs that made up the small lobby space. She slipped the blazer from her uniform off of her shoulders and placed it on the seat of the chair next to her, before patting it with her hand.

"Come here," she said and Mary Ellis obeyed, sinking down in the chair next to her, "Don't lean back against the chair." When Mary Ellis was settled, she continued, "Where are you heading?"

For a moment, Mary Ellis's head flickered with images of Dylan. His chilling smile. The way he snatched at the map, tried to withhold it from her. Then, in a moment, her thoughts shifted to Charles. The way he was able to take over her life so quickly. His tight grip on her shoulders. But where else did she have to turn? Slouching, Mary Ellis passed the map to Bobby, who spread it out, frowning.

"It is my day off tomorrow. I will take you." She looked up to meet Mary Ellis's eyes, searching for a nod of confirmation, but Mary Ellis stayed still.

"I don't want to-"

"I don't want the police poking around here when you get killed hitchhiking, so I will take you." Bobby's fists were balled in her lap, her face hard and back straight. "Tonight you can stay in my room, I'll bring up a cot from the basement."

"No," Mary Ellis stammered. "I can't stay with you." Bobby's brow came together, then her features softened.

"Room 210 is available. You can stay there as long as no one comes to rent it tonight. I'll bring a cot up so you don't mess up the bed."

Mary Ellis felt tears rim her eyes. Though anxiety hovered on the edges of her mind, coupled with stabs of images of Charles and Dylan, Mary Ellis just wanted to have someone else take care of her. She wanted this to be out of her control.

When she eventually nodded, Bobby returned to the her place behind front desk and retrieved the key for room 210 from the board with pegs where every room key was hung. In a single motion, she tossed it to Mary Ellis.

"I will be up with the cot in a couple of minutes, but for now head on up there yourself. It's on the second floor, all the way at the end of the building." Then, almost as an afterthought, "Don't mess anything up."

Mary Ellis took the keys from her hand without another word. She turned and exited the motel once again, barely able to climb to the second story of the building and walk to the end of the hall. Still, she made it after what seemed like an eternity.

As she pushed open the door to the tiny room, Mary Ellis finally felt safe. She crept into the center of the room and stood still, wanting all at once to collapse on the floor and sleep and to wait up all night, making sure that no one would come after her.

After a few minutes Bobby returned, carrying a small blue cot and a stack of blankets. She set them out on the floor and glanced around the room before her gaze turned to Mary Ellis.

"You should set your clothes out in the bathroom so that they get dry." When Mary Ellis said nothing she continued, "You should try to get some sleep. I'll see you tomorrow. Goodnight."

Mary Ellis stayed silent and Bobby took a deep breath. Then she turned and left the room. Mary Ellis was finally alone.

She wanted to curl up on the carpet, to immediately collapse under the weight of her body, but Mary Ellis knew that she should follow Bobby's instructions. In a daze, she carried her bags into the bathroom and began spreading the clothes inside out onto every available surface. When she was finished, Mary Ellis stripped, draping her last wet clothes over the toilet seat. Then she stumbled back into the bedroom and nearly fell onto the cot, pulling the blankets tight around her, but sleep came only in short spurts that night, Mary Ellis being awakened every hour or so with a jolt of fear. She was so close to the end of her journey, the moment where she could finally see clearly who her parents are. When she could finally know where the rest of her life would lead.

***

Mary Ellis awoke the next morning to a pounding on the motel room's door.

"Hey, kid, it's me," a voice called.

For a minute, Mary Ellis was frazzled, her heart began to beat quickly as she tried to remember where she was, but her mind soon returned to her.

"I'll be there in a second," Mary Ellis said, rushing into the bathroom. As quick as she could, she selected the driest clothes available and pulled them on. Then she rushed back to the door and pulled it open.

In front of her, Bobby stood in plain clothes. Her straight, brown hair was pulled back into a wispy ponytail and she wore a flannel button-up and baggy jeans.

"If you come downstairs, I'll make you something to eat."

"I still need to pack my bag."

"Meet me downstairs, then, when you're finished. I'm in the room to the right of the door." When Mary Ellis nodded, Bobby swirled around and started down the stairs, shutting the door behind her.

When she was gone, Mary Ellis entered the bathroom and began shoving her clothes into the bag at random. She finished quickly and started towards the lobby. The rain continued, now more of a drizzle than the torrent it had been for the past couple of days, but it barely bothered Mary Ellis after her days in the rain.

She went quickly to Bobby's room, skirting around the edge of the lobby and slipping into the first room down the hall. Bobby's apartment was as tiny as the other motel rooms but with an attached kitchen, which seemed almost smashed into the corner.

Bobby was leaned over the stove, scrambling eggs. When Mary Ellis opened the door, she could hear Bobby humming, but the moment Bobby realized that Mary Ellis had arrived the humming stopped.

"Do you have the address of where you're heading?" Bobby asked. She spun around, placing a plate in front of Mary Ellis that was full of scrambled eggs. "I hope you'll eat this, cause I don't cook much."

"Thank you," Mary Ellis mumbled, taking the fork that Bobby passed to her.

Bobby leaned against the counter. "I don't know if I want to know your story, but if you want to offer it up I'd hear it."

"I really am going to my parents' house."

"Uh-huh," Bobby said, sounding unconvinced, "as long as it's a safe place."

"It is." Mary Ellis was shoveling eggs into her mouth, staring down at her plate, rather than into Bobby's eyes.

"I'm going to check with your parents to make sure. I'll be right back, I'm heading to the bathroom." Bobby entered the bathroom, leaving Mary Ellis to sit with her thoughts.

For the moment, Mary Ellis merely felt resigned. She couldn't take even another couple of days of walking, especially in the cold of the rain. There was a slight bit of fear in her heart: fear that Bobby would hurt her or that she wouldn't take her right to her parents apartment, but there was no better option than the one she had now.

Eventually, Bobby entered again, a bag slung over her shoulder. "Are you sure there's no one you can call? To make sure you have a place to go."

"I don't think I should." Mary Ellis stood up.

"Why not?"

"Because. They don't know I'm coming."

Bobby stared down at Mary Ellis for a moment, frowning.

"Call them." Bobby retrieved the phone from the other side of the room and passed it to Mary Ellis. "Now. I'll go out into the lobby."

Mary Ellis nodded, dialing the numbers, as Bobby passed by her and left through the front door. She didn't care anymore, just wanting to be told what to do, what choices to make. She pressed the call button.

The phone rang once. Then twice.

"Hello?" The voice on the other end of the line was gruff and gravely. Mary Ellis didn't think she could speak.

"Hello?" the voice asked again, irritation creeping into her voice.

"Uh, hi. It's me, Mary Ellis." There was silence for a moment.

"Honey, I think you have the wrong number."

"Uh-uh. You're Rachel Walker. I found your number in the White Pages."

"I don't think-"

"Say it's you. Please don't lie to me."

"I really didn't think you'd be stupid enough to- When they called I didn't think..."

"What?" Mary Ellis gripped the phone, white-knuckled, bouncing from foot to foot.

"Where are you right now?"

"I'm in North Carolina. At a motel." Mary Ellis looked around, anxiety creeping into her. The room was completely empty.

"Alone?"

"Gran's dead," Mary Ellis said, and once again silence hummed on the other end of the line.

"I know. Does anyone know you've made it here?"

"Only you." For a moment, Mary Ellis considered telling the whole story, explaining each and every person who helped her reach the point where she was. Who helped her. Who hurt her.

"What's your address?" Mary Ellis glanced around again.

"What?"

"Where are you? What is the address of the place where you are staying right now?"

Mary Ellis could feel herself shaking. "One second," she said, placing the phone onto the counter and rushing out into the lobby.

"What's the address of this place?" she asked Bobby, who told her.

Mary Ellis ran back into the room, relaying the information back into the phone.

"I'll be there as soon as I can be. Don't leave," The woman sighed and hung up before Mary Ellis could reply.

Mary Ellis placed the phone onto its dock and entered back into the lobby. She slunk back towards Bobby and sat down in the spinning chair which Bobby stood next to. The lobby was empty.

"You ready to go?" Bobby asked, ignoring Mary Ellis's apparent anxiety.

Mary Ellis spun around in the chair, staring at the floor.

"I'm not going with you."

Bobby furrowed her brow. "Where are you going then?" she chuckled.

"My mom's coming to pick me up." Mary Ellis kicked at the floor.

Bobby placed her hand on the arm of the chair and squatted down to be eye level with Mary Ellis. "You sure you okay, kid?" Bobby reached out and squeezed her hand. "I'm going to talk to your mom okay."

Mary Ellis nodded.

"Okay," Bobby said, standing back up.

Mary Ellis stared up at her for a moment, then stood up. She walked into the room for a moment to grab her bags and then returned awkwardly to the center of the lobby's seating area watching the minute hand of the clock hanging on the far wall slowly slip forward. A family of people entered at one point, the parents dragging three kids of varying ages, bringing commotion into the room as the man attempted to check in with a little girl hanging off of his arm and the woman struggled to wrangle the other two children into seats. Sometime during the clatter, a man in a suit passed through the lobby, not even glancing at the checkout desk.

About forty minutes after Mary Ellis made the call, Mary Ellis now sunk down into the lobby's seats, the doors slid open and a woman passed through them. She was tall with peroxide blonde hair that fell like limp ramen around her shoulders and thick eyeliner, smudged from the rain. The woman glanced around the lobby for a moment and Mary Ellis's heart leapt. The woman locked eyes with her and began to cross the room.

"Mary Ellis?" she huffed, grabbing the little girl's shoulder.

Mary Ellis nodded.

"We're going to head to my place so we can talk about what's going to happen from here on out, okay?"

"Wait," Bobby said, crossing the lobby to grab, Rachel's arm. She practically dragged her across the lobby, stopping just out of Mary Ellis's earshot.

They spoke for a few moments, Bobby seeming increasingly angry. Mary Ellis couldn't read Rachel's face. Eventually, though, they returned to stare down at Mary Ellis. Rachel eventually said, "you ready to go?"

It didn't seem much like a question to Mary Ellis, but she still piped out a yes and followed her mother back out into the rain.

Moving quickly, her mother passed by lines of cars to the very back of the lot. She opened first the passenger side door of a sagging black pickup then walked around to the driver's side and climbed in. Mary Ellis clambered in and shut the door. The inside of the car was littered with fast food wrappers and receipts. Mary Ellis nudged something plastic with her toes as she climbed into the car and caught a glimpse of something metal, but didn't explore what it was. When she was sitting in the seat, she was silent for a moment, listening to the rain beat down on the car's windows. This didn't feel like her mother's car; this person didn't feel like her mother. But it was, she was. Mary Ellis didn't know what she could do except follow along.

"Come on. Buckle up." Her mother nudged her slightly.

Mary Ellis fondled for her seatbelt and then clicked it into place, but she could feel her heart thundering in her chest. Her hands were shaking.

"Okay, I'm ready," Mary Ellis let silence fill the cab, unsure of what to call her mother. She wanted to say mom, like she did years ago, but something stopped her.

"I guess you know I'm Rachel."

Mary Ellis nodded and Rachel pulled out of her spot, easing out into traffic.

"So," Rachel started, "I know what brings you here."

"Gran died. I didn't have anyone to stay with."

Rachel sighed, keeping her eyes completely focused on traffic.

"I guess you can stay with me until we figure out what to do with you." Rachel wove through traffic, going faster than Mary Ellis ever had with Gran. As she did, Mary Ellis stared at her, trying to match the image she had of her young mother with her mother now. Her bright smile and kind eyes had sagged and warped under the hand of time and the nearly threadbare T-shirt she was wearing didn't match Mary Ellis's internal image of her mother. Even the shake of the woman's hand was new to Mary Ellis, though she thought it may have been there the whole time and she had just never noticed it in youth. In fact, Mary Ellis could have guessed this was a whole new woman. Instead of Mom, she's now Rachel, who spoke very little and drove too fast and didn't care at all what her car looked like.

As Rachel swerved past a couple in a red convertible, all of the garbage on the floor of the truck slid to the side, revealing a whole new layer of things. Amongst more wrappers and receipts, a single black glove, and a small stack of magazines, a disposable cellphone was sitting on the floor. Mary Ellis contemplated picking it up for a moment, just staring at it. Slowly, she reached down, feeling the seat belt cut into her stomach and grabbed it.

"Don't touch that," Rachel shouted, and Mary Ellis let go of the phone.

"What is it for?"

"Nothing you need to worry about."

"What if I need to make a call?" Mary Ellis asked, tucking her feet up onto the seat in order to avoid stepping on it.

"Who would you have to call?" Rachel didn't even turn to glance at Mary Ellis, totally focused on the road.

Rachel eased into a parking lot next to a series of duplexes. Parking, Rachel climbed out of the car and walked to the other side, ready to open the door, but Mary Ellis had already opened it herself and was standing next to the car.

"Come on," Rachel said awkwardly, holding out her hand. Hesitating, Mary Ellis took it and they walked up to Rachel's doorway. When they reached it, Rachel held open the door, letting Mary Ellis go in front of her.

The tight hallway was lined with dust bunnies and an aged carpet that seemed ill-fitting for the place where it sat. Nothing about the hallway stirred anything in Mary Ellis, so she pushed down the hallway into the living room.

"Mary Ellis," Rachel said, following quickly after her.

Mary Ellis didn't pay attention, just passed into the living room. It was nothing like the apartment she lived in when she was young. It was filled with modern, clean looking furniture, though the room was actually cluttered with magazines and old food.

"Come on," Rachel said, watching Mary Ellis's face fall upon seeing the room, "you can put your stuff in the guest room." She led Mary Ellis through another hallway and opened the door, letting her enter. As she did, Mary Ellis placed her bag on the floor. Rachel had her own guest room. For a moment, Mary Ellis tried to picture what her old bedroom locked like. The pale pink of the walls and the posters of kids television shows that were taped to the walls. When she opened her eyes again, Mary Ellis was back in the dark bedroom, with boxes stacked up against one of the walls.

"Sorry about all the shit," Rachel said, trying to quickly clean the boxes off of the bed, stacking them higher along the wall.

Mary Ellis just watched her.

"It's all I have" Rachel suddenly seemed self-conscious.

"Sorry," Mary Ellis mumbled

Rachel shifted from foot to foot.

"Do you need anything?"

Mary Ellis frowned. "I'm fine."

Rachel walked out of the room then, shutting the door behind her. When she was gone, Mary Ellis just stood in the center of the room. After a little while, Mary Ellis could hear Rachel talking on the phone in the living room. That jolted Mary Ellis slightly, and she walked over to the bed. She sat down and took in everything around her: the stacks of boxes left completely unlabeled, a stack of old clothing shoved into the corner. She couldn't even open the closet doors if she wanted to, not that she was supposed to unpack. Instead, she just stared at her bags.

Mary Ellis walked over to the pile of old clothes, T-shirts from what looked like local bands, jean shorts that looked far too big for her, a belt that she could wear cinched at her waist. The belt too was too big, so her father had cut a new hole a couple inches past where they had originally ended. Her father... Mary Ellis stood up once again, walking out into the living room, where Rachel was just putting the phone back into her pocket.

"Rachel?" Mary Ellis asked, and Rachel nodded.

"Is my dad ever going to come here?"

Rachel's eyes went wide and she reached for the table.

"Your father, he-" she wouldn't meet Mary Ellis's eyes. "He passed away two years ago." Mary Ellis wanted to run back into her bedroom, but something kept her feet stuck to the floor.

"What happened?" she asked quietly.

"He was sick, honey. For a long time."

"Oh." Mary Ellis stared at the carpet, feeling a heat growing behind her eyes.

"I'm really sorry."

Suddenly, Mary Ellis was hyperaware of the actions of Rachel, who was sorting awkwardly through a stack of junk mail. Mary Ellis squeezed her eyes shut, trying to blink away the tears, but they burned down her face. Rachel just stared at her for a moment, then took a few small steps towards Mary Ellis, holding her arms out. Mary Ellis stayed glued to her spot on the carpet. Rachel put her arms down and stopped moving, turning her gaze towards the floor.

"He was happy when he died." Rachel said then after a moment. "It was hard on me too."

Mary Ellis just nodded slightly.

"We used to go everywhere together, you know. He was my entire world."

Mary Ellis swiped at the fat tears on her face, suddenly feeling betrayed.

"You never gave me that chance."

"It's better that you didn't know him. Don't know me," Rachel said again, weakly. There was something about the way that she said it that made Mary Ellis uncomfortable, so she turned away. Rachel began to say something else but Mary Ellis just walked into her bedroom, shutting the door.

She picked up her bags and brought them to the bed, already beginning to tear them open. There was no trace of her father in the room. The bed shook as she lay crying, thinking of the letters she'd lost, the last piece of him she'd had. Even her mother looked like something else, something she had never seen before. Gone were the dreams of the perfect family, now there was only Rachel. Rachel whose once soft dark brown hair had been bleached to a harsh blonde. Whose skin now sagged under her eyes and creased when she smiled. Who looked almost like a skeleton.

"Mary Ellis?" Rachel knocked on the door lightly and Mary Ellis turned over. A moment passed.

Mary Ellis stared at the door. After another moment, she pushed it open.

"I need a minute," Mary Ellis tried to sit up, swiping at the tears in her eyes.

Rachel stopped moving and stood in the doorway, leaning against the door frame.

"Are you going to be okay?"

Mary Ellis just stared at her, squinting. She scoffed.

"You know I don't want to do this to you." Rachel smiled slightly, it seemed fake.

"Sure, whatever."

"But this is what it has to be."

Mary Ellis was silent.

Mary Ellis wanted to lurch at her for taking this so lightly.

"That's why I think it might be best if we call the police to make sure you get somewhere you can be safe."

At this, Mary Ellis leapt up.

"Why can't I be safe here?"

"You're so young I don't think you'd understand..." Rachel fondled her arm. Mary Ellis noticed it was peppered with tiny scars.

"I just turned eleven."

"I know, honey. I'm sorry."

"They're not going to send me anywhere nice. They didn't before."

Rachel took a shaky breath.

"I know you don't understand-"

"Then make me understand. Explain it to me."

"I can't. I'm sorry."

"I'm not stupid. You abandoned me the last time without even telling me what you were doing."

"I-I-"

"It hurts! It really fucking hurts, because I've been waiting for you, both of you, for such a long time and now I get here and you just want to send me back."

"Why do you think we left in the first place?"

"Gran said you and Daddy had an accident and were sick, but you would get better eventually. You seem fine, so why won't you take me?"

Rachel's hands were shaking.

"I don't know how to explain this to you, but I'm not fine. If I was fine I would have come back for you."

"Are you not even trying then?"

"Trying for what?"

"To get better. To be fine so that I can come and stay with you again. Do you even care what is happening to me?"

"Mary Ellis..."

"You don't!"

"I do. I promise I do, that's why I left. I know it's really hard to understand how that would be possible."

"Then explain it to me."

"No!" Rachel said, scowling, "you're too young to know about these kinds of things." Rachel was trying to get Mary Ellis to step out into the living room but she wouldn't leave the guest room. From Mary Ellis's pocket, Gran's phone began to ring.

"I'm going to get this," Mary Ellis said.

Rachel glanced around the room, searching for Mary Ellis's eyes. Mary Ellis wouldn't meet her gaze. When Rachel realized the conversation was over she just nodded once again and slipped out of the room, leaving her daughter alone.

Mary Ellis stared at her hands, which were folded in her lap. The air in the apartment seemed dead and hung like a weight around her. Since the door was slightly open, Mary Ellis crossed the room and pulled the door shut, sinking onto the ground. She tried to find something familiar in the space around her, some scrap of the life she once led. Her thoughts could only trail to her last memories of her family though, and she let herself get lost in it for a moment.

***

Young Mary Ellis mashed the box in her hands, pulling the straw out. At first she froze where Rachel had left her on the floor, only moving when anxiety had begun to build in her. Then she waited, occasionally playing with her box or her other toys, occasionally sleeping, occasionally crying. By the time the sun set, neither of her parents had arrived home. Mary Ellis clambered into her bed, tucked herself in, and went to sleep. Over the next few days this process continued: filling her days with nothing of substance, trying to cobble together a meal, then sleeping. It was more than four days and Mary Ellis was still alone. She was still trying her hardest to retain a life.

* * *

She remembered how it felt to be alone for such a long time, only in a lonely ache. She remembered the final night before social services came, curling herself up in one of her father's old T-shirts, sobbing into the fabric of the shirt until it was nearly soaked. Mary Ellis remembered the door finally opening, and her head peeking up to see her parents finally home again. She remembered the let down when it was someone else.

Mary Ellis stood up, angry, and flung the door of the guest room open. She watched Rachel for a moment, who was still sitting on the sofa, talking on the phone. Rachel's eyes met Mary Ellis's as she was hanging up and she placed the phone down on the table.

"How could you let them take me?"

Rachel's face contorted and changed.

"Mary Ellis, I didn't have any other choice."

"You could have taken care of me. You could have let me have a normal home, lived with a normal person.

"Your life was better with your grandmother. Better without me." Rachel was now bent over, staring at her hands in her lap.

"No, it hurt me. Gran hated me; she didn't want me. You just abandoned me because you didn't want to take care of me."

"I'm sorry." Rachel looked up at her daughter, reaching out her hand towards her. Mary Ellis didn't move to take it.

"You just took the opportunity to pawn me off at whatever chance you could get. You didn't want me."

"It's more complicated than that."

"Whatever." The room was filled with a long, loud silence.

"Do you at least understand why you can't stay now?"

Mary Ellis sighed, averting her eyes from her mother. Rachel stood up, staring down at her.

"Listen."

"Don't talk to me like that."

Rachel stared past Mary Ellis at the television.

"I'm sorry."

"I'm going back to my room."

Rachel just nodded. Mary Ellis stood up and left the room, slamming her door behind her as she entered. She sank to the ground, tears beginning to spill from her eyes. Her mind flickered to home, Pennsylvania, where she once longed to leave, now seemed so wonderful. She missed Stacy's tiny voice and the things they once did together. Mary Ellis knew she could leave here. She could go somewhere else and stay alone, live on the streets and on the money she had and then... Mary Ellis didn't know, but it would be better than being here for another moment, reminded of all of the things that she was losing. She considered it. If she tried and social services got her it would just end up the same as if she stayed, so it was worth a shot. At this point anything was worth it.

Slowly, Mary Ellis stood up and got her bags from the other side of the room. She left her room. As she opened the door she glanced around, the living room was empty. For what she thought would be the last time, Mary Ellis took in Rachel's home: the small, cluttered coffee table, the cramped kitchen that could be seen slightly through a small window in the wall that separated the two rooms from each other, the worn sofa. This place was what she worked for for so long. It had shifted in her mind though, there was no home for her, nowhere that was truly her own. Mary Ellis shook herself out of her thoughts and walked to the door, opening it as quietly as she could. She waited just one more moment, then walked out.

She ran, down the steps of the house and out into the street. Then she stopped. Mary Ellis had never walked these streets before. Taking a minute to orient herself, Mary Ellis caught sight of a bus stop and started down the street, the last of the nostalgia fading from her mind, at least for that moment.

Stopping at the bus stop Mary Ellis sank down onto the bench. She had no idea when the next bus was coming or where it went, but she needed to go. So, Mary Ellis waited. And waited more when the bus didn't come. The sun had begun to sink over the horizon and Mary Ellis realized how long it had been since she'd slept comfortably, since she was able to embrace her own bed. Letting her eyes hang half shut, Mary Ellis slumped against the bench, sure that the coming of the bus would wake her up.

"Where have you been?" A frustrated voice shook Mary Ellis out of her sleep.

Opening her eyes, she could see Rachel standing in front of her.

"I'm going," Mary Ellis muttered, sinking lower onto the bench.

"Where? Where can you go?"

Mary Ellis sat up, swiping the sleep from her eyes and frowning.

"I don't know. If I can't stay here, I don't want to go back with social services again."

"So what? You're going to get a job. You know you can't get a job at eleven, right?"

"I'll figure something out. You don't have to worry about it."

"Of course, I have to worry I'm your-"

"No. No, you don't get that excuse. You didn't worry about me for six years and if I didn't come to find you you wouldn't be worrying now."

"I can't just let a kid roam the streets alone."

"Why do you care?"

Rachel wouldn't make eye contact with Mary Ellis.

"What? Do you just not want to get in trouble? Well, I won't tell on you and no one will know I was here, just let me go."

"I can't do that."

"It shouldn't be hard, you've done it before."

"Mary Ellis..." Rachel said and at that moment a bus slid up to the stop, its doors flinging open. Mary Ellis stood up suddenly and walked towards the doorway. As she stepped on the first stair, Rachel grabbed Mary Ellis's arm, trying to wretch her back onto the pavement. Mary Ellis struggled to pull her arm away.

"Just let go of me. Let me leave you alone like you want."

"I can't just let you wander alone."

Mary Ellis pulled her arm away and marched up the stairs, thrusting a couple of dollars at the bus's driver.

"Sorry, kid, I don't think your mother wants you to go."

Mary Ellis sighed, keeping her arm outstretched the money clutched in her fist.

"She's not my mom."

Rachel was coming up the stairs.

"You liar," Rachel said, grabbing back onto Mary Ellis.

"Stop," Mary Ellis said in a strange, strangled manner. Rachel picked her up and began to remove her from the bus. Mary Ellis caught a glimpse of the other passengers on the bus staring at her.

Rachel placed Mary Ellis on the sidewalk when they reached the bottom of the stairs. The bus driver peered at them for a moment, clearly uncomfortable, but then he began to pull away. Mary Ellis let out a cry.

"You're not going and that's final."

"Then let me stay with you." Mary Ellis knew she was being too loud, knew she was probably screaming, but she didn't care.

Rachel stared at her.

"You know I can't."

Mary Ellis reeled back, heading a little too far into the street.

"This is bullshit," she screamed, feeling the eyes of passersby on her, feeling like a brat. Then both women fell silent, breathing heavily. Mary Ellis felt a car whisk past her, her shirt fluttering in the wind, and turned to face the street. Suddenly, she felt Rachel's arm, gentler now, guide her back to the sidewalk.

"I've never been a good mother to you," Rachel started.

Mary Ellis scoffed, but could feel a hurt in the back of her throat. It burned her. Suddenly, Mary Ellis felt like she was on the verge of tears.

"And I know that even now, even if I tried my hardest, I could never be the person you want me to be." Rachel paused, as if to give Mary Ellis a moment to speak, but Mary Ellis stayed silent, staring at the shoes of the people passing by her.

"That's why you can't stay with me. Going back to your home you would at least have the chance to have guardians who can adequately care for you."

"But I want you," Mary Ellis muttered, not looking up. She felt far from here, the street, other people, all seemed distant. All Mary Ellis could hear was the sound of her mother's voice and the heave of her heavy breaths.

"You want a mother. I can't be that for you. Come on."

Mary Ellis stood, considering.

"Fine." Mary Ellis shook Rachel off. As Rachel started towards her building once again, Mary Ellis followed her. Mary Ellis thought she heard Rachel saying something, but she wasn't listening. Instead, she was swimming in her head, her now seemingly sealed fate looming over her. She went back up the stairs and through the door, and before she knew it, Mary Ellis was standing in the guest room once again. It was a completely vacant and empty room, and even if it meant something, that meaning was now destroyed. Mary Ellis felt adrift, afraid for herself. She had no one, nowhere. Her home was gone and now she didn't even have the idea that there was a perfect life waiting for her.

Mary Ellis just shut the door and crept into bed. She pulled the blankets around herself and tried to shut her mind off and go back to sleep, but it was early and there was nothing she could do but lay in bed and think.

After a few minutes, the door to her bedroom swung slightly open and Rachel stuck her head in. She was holding a peanut butter and jelly sandwich on a plate, which she placed on the floor right inside the doorway. Then closed the door without another word. Without a goodnight. Mary Ellis was done eating peanut butter sandwiches, sick of all of the ones she had on the journey, so she left it sitting by the door.

Mary Ellis tried her hardest to sink into sleep, but it didn't seem like it was coming. Even Gran, who was harsh and uncaring, had taken Mary Ellis in when she had nowhere else to go, but her mother was going to abandon her once again. She kept her safe in her home, but now, here, Mary Ellis couldn't be sure of what she had or where she would be staying.

She lay on the bed with eyes half open, trying to weight down her mind into sleep. Her head still swam with images of that afternoon's fight or her mother's arms around her wrists guiding her back towards the house, what should be her home. Tomorrow everything would be over, they wouldn't be ending the night in a screaming match about who was right.

As the night went on, Mary Ellis's dense thoughts began to dissipate and give way to the lightness of sleep. Mary Ellis felt like she was floating, up and out of her head, and drifted away into a dream.

She awoke the next morning to light filtering through the blinds on the wall next to her. In the kitchen she could hear movement, what sounded like the clinking of glass and the hum of a microwave. Mary Ellis stood up and crossed the room, opening the door quietly into the living room.

Immediately, Mary Ellis could see her mother hunched over the kitchen counter. Her small sloping shoulders were hunched over a glass bowl with eggs in it, already thoroughly mixed. As she approached, Rachel gave Mary Ellis a small, tight-lipped smile.

"I'm just making breakfast. It should be a little while."

"That's fine. I can wait." Mary Ellis tried to put on her most convincing grin and sunk down onto the sofa. She sat for a moment, unsure of what to do with her hands. Rachel was sweeping around the room, making much more noise than Gran used to when she would cook for Mary Ellis.

"Do you want me to turn on the television for you?" Rachel asked, looking up from a pan for a moment.

Mary Ellis nodded, when Rachel didn't respond she said, "Yes, please." The TV flickered to life and displayed a news channel, blaring things that Mary Ellis couldn't care less about. She watched the man on the screen for a moment, seeing his mouth flapping up and down without hearing the words he was saying. Photos of the current news appeared next to his head, but his voice drifted in and out of Mary Ellis's memory without consequence or even understanding.

She wanted to ask Rachel if they could watch something different. Typically this would be the time that Looney Toons was on and that was Mary Ellis's favorite, but she couldn't be a burden. With her mother moving through the kitchen so calmly, Mary Ellis didn't want to show that she would be an imposition to her. That is if Rachel didn't ship her off before she got a chance to show how she could be an asset.

At some point the TV turned off and Mary Ellis felt Rachel sink onto the sofa beside her. As soon as Rachel was settled she thrust a plate with a piece of toast and eggs into Mary Ellis's hands. Mary Ellis stared down at them for a moment. It was slightly burnt.

Rachel glanced at the ceiling for a moment, seemingly trying to work up her nerve for something.

"We need to talk," she said. Mary Ellis wanted to nod, but her head stayed still. Instead, her knee began to bounce up and down. "I'm just going to tell you flat out what is going to happen from here on. Is that alright?"

This time Mary Ellis nodded.

"Tomorrow someone will come to pick you up."

"But-"

"Please don't."

"I know what you think you're doing, but you are just leaving me to have a shitty life. You say life will suck if I stay with you, but life will suck anyways, so just take me in." Mary Ellis could feel her cheeks heating up. She could hear birds chirping outside of the apartment's tiny windows, but it only increased her frustration at Rachel.

"Just. Stop," Rachel muttered, staring into her lap as the conversation lapsed into silence. Mary Ellis wanted Rachel to feel her eyes burning into her. To crush her with the weight of the conversation into submitting to her wishes, but Rachel just stayed silent. Mary Ellis wanted to move, to leave the apartment, but she couldn't let Rachel win. She couldn't give up with the fact that she wanted to stay with her mother.

"Listen, I got here didn't I. I can clearly take care of myself. If you just let me stay here I'll take care of myself here. I can even get a job if you need me to."

"This isn't something worth fighting about."

"I need to make a phone call." Mary Ellis didn't know what she was feeling, emotions just kind of swarmed around her swirling through her body. She thought she was being mature, at least she was trying her hardest to be, but she couldn't help feeling that Rachel was just treating her like she was stupid.

Mary Ellis walked out into the silence of the empty street, able to hear Rachel's muffled voice from inside the house. Above her, Mary Ellis could hear footsteps and the far off sound of an argument somewhere in the complex. The air around her hung still though, blanketing Mary Ellis in a kind of calmness. Gone was her frantic need to escape or her need to return to North Carolina; now she was only floating through the present, unconcerned with the past or future. Whatever happened next, Mary Ellis now knew that something in her life was going to change. She guessed that she knew this from the start, but when she began her journey this was not the ending she expected. Nostalgia twisted in her gut, sending a flurry of images of Stacy into her mind. What would become of them?

Though it was only a few days prior Mary Ellis had heard her best friend's voice, she suddenly felt that she needed to call her. She sunk down onto the bus bench outside of Rachel's house and pulled her phone out of her pocket. The phone had barely rung when someone picked it up.

"Hello?" The voice on the other end of the line wasn't Stacy's; it sounded like a gruff man. Stacy's father? Mary Ellis wasn't sure what to do.

"Mary Ellis?" the man asked again. Mary Ellis placed the phone back on the hook. Her mind began to feel weak. She couldn't even have contact with her best friend If she wanted to. There was only one more number she could call. She dug in her bag for the piece of paper and input the number quickly into the phone. It rang once.

"Hello?" the bright voice of Jess almost laughed into the phone.

"Jess? It's me, Mary Ellis."

"Oh hi, how are you?" Mary Ellis leaned down to settle herself on the pavement, ensuring she was avoiding any gum that was stuck to the ground.

"I'm okay." Mary Ellis thought her voice might be wavering. "I was just calling to let you guys know that I'm with my mom. We're all good."

"Are you sure?"

For a moment, Mary Ellis just nodded. Then, realizing what she was doing, she muttered, "yeah."

"Do you need anything?"

"Nope I just wanted to make sure you knew. Your dad asked me to call."

"I asked you to call too, silly. How was your trip?"

A man passing by Mary Ellis, going to sit on the bus bench next to her, scowled in her direction. She mouthed "sorry" and clutched the phone closer to her head.

"It was boring. What have you been up to?"

"Me and a couple of kids turned the rope swing we went on into a tire swing, now it's easier for some of the little kids to hold on. We also got kicked out of the ice cream shop, because Margret's brother almost got fired for giving us free stuff. We've gotta start going to the corner store that Ollie's family owns. We're also going to try to build a clubhouse for all of the kids in the neighborhood out of scrap wood and metal we find."

Mary Ellis smiled, relishing in the benign-ness of the story and all of its players. That was why she was caught off guard when Jess finally broke the stream of gossip.
"Are you and your parents planning to do anything soon?"

Mary Ellis sighed.

Trying to put on her best happy voice, Mary Ellis said, "Yeah, my mom and I are going to the zoo later. We went out to dinner last night and it was so delicious. We're going out to pick out new clothes for the next school year in a couple of weeks." Mary Ellis stopped, catching her breath.

"That sounds great."

"Yeah." Silence hung around them.

"I have to get ready to go somewhere with my mom, okay? We can talk later."

"Alright," Mary Ellis practically croaked. The phone line went dead. Mary Ellis hung the phone back up on the hook. She had nothing to do not, but go back to the house.

***

The next morning she was woken up earlier. The night before she had headed back up to the house and locked herself into her room until she fell asleep. Now, Mary Ellis was sitting up in her bed, watching as who she could only assume was Rachel, pounded on her door.

"Mary Ellis, you need to get up."

"I'm up," Mary Ellis called, shuffling out of bed and into the bathroom. Pushing past Rachel without a word to her.

"They'll be here in thirty minutes."

Mary Ellis's heart sunk. She had hoped that her mother would have reconsidered or forgotten or would tell Mary Ellis that she was free to try to make it on her own. But no.

Mary Ellis sulked to the bathroom and climbed into the shower, keeping the water cool so as not to irritate her sunburn. She stood under the water, washing her hair and staring down at the drain. She was trying not to think.

Chapter Twenty-Two

Once again, Stacy was sitting at her kitchen table when the call arrived. As she stood up to grab the phone, Stacy's father rushed into the room past her to get it first. He waited for a long time before speaking.

"That's wonderful news," her father was leaning against the wall. There was no smile on his face.

"What do you think is going to happen to her?" Stacy watched her father's furrowed brow. She quietly shut the book that she was reading and stepped towards her father. He was nodding along to someone on the other side of the phone.

"Well, if you need someone to take her for a little while everything gets figured out, we'd be happy to." Just a moment. "Well, not directly, but Stacy's her best friend. Her only friend I think."

"Thank you so much. Just let us know if you need anything." Stacy's father placed the phone back on its hook. He walked to where Stacy was standing, seeming to tower over her.

"They found her." Stacy's eyes bulged, even though she could have guessed. "She's probably going to stay here for a little while while social services figures out what is going to happen to her."

"Great." Stacy didn't know what to think. What had happened to her that they had gotten ahold of her but she wasn't with her mother? Where had she gone? Was she okay? Was she the same?

"Where did they find her?"

"They said she went to live with her mother."

"So why is she coming here?" Stacy's voice was a whisper. Her father looked down at her, gripping Stacy's shoulder.

He smiled a grim smile, which wavered only slightly as he said, "Mary Ellis's mother is not fit to take care of her. They are driving up here together so she can drop Mary Ellis off. They're going to have to find some other family member she can stay with."

"Why can't she just live with us?" Stacy's eyes were wide as saucers, but her father just pressed his lips together.

"I haven't even spoken to your mother about this yet, Stacy."

"Why don't you go do that?" Stacy gathered her things from the table and started upstairs. "I need to get my room ready anyways."

Stacy walked upstairs to her bedroom and placed her things onto her bed. She began to pick things up from her floor, placing them onto the proper shelf or into the right drawer. She made a small bed on the floor out of pillows and blankets, even though it wasn't going to be needed for a couple of days.

Mary Ellis was coming home.

Chapter Twenty-Three

The last few days had been nothing. Absolutely nothing. Two days earlier Rachel and Mary Ellis had stood in front of each other for the last time, waiting inside while the social service worker that had come for Mary Ellis readied the car.

"Come on, kid, it's time," Rachel said, nudging her towards the door as the social service worker opened it. As they reached the door though, Rachel stopped.

"Wait, hold up. I need to talk to the kid." Rachel raised her hand to silence the social service worker who stepped forward to talk to her, instead leaning down to talk to Mary Ellis. She kneeled in front of her daughter, placing a hand on her cheek, with the other hand she swept a piece of Mary Ellis's hair out of her face, coiling it around her finger. "I'm really hate to do this you know."

Mary Ellis stared blankly ahead, her eyes focused on a spot past Rachel's shoulder.

"You're my daughter and no matter what, I love you."

Mary Ellis shifted her gaze to look at the floor. As Rachel watched her, tears began to spill onto her cheeks, she wiped them away as they came.

Rachel smiled. "You're going to be a resourceful woman, just like me."

Finally, Mary Ellis opened her mouth, in the most pitiful croak Mary Ellis thought she had ever heard she muttered, "I don't want to be like you." The tears were falling faster and faster, Mary Ellis let them linger on her cheeks. Rachel sighed and looked away from Mary Ellis, she gave her cheek a little squeeze.

"See you, kid."

＊

When Mary Ellis and the worker reached the edge of Parkville, the tension in Mary Ellis rose. There was nothing left for her to do but leave. There was nothing left for her to say that could convince them to take her back to her mother. She sat crouched in the back seat of the car, waiting to be dropped off at the police station where she would inevitably be pushed around for a long time. Where she would never settle down.

It was only a few minutes before they slid into the police station's parking lot. They parked the car in the corner of the lot, as far as she could be from any of the other cars that were parked there.

The social services worker pushed herself out of the car, walking around it's circumference to open up the door for Mary Ellis. Together, they walked through the parking lot and into the stations front door, the worker staring straight ahead, Mary Ellis examining the cloudy sky.

Inside they were met by a swarm of officer's who immediately began to pepper Mary Ellis with questions. Someone took Mary Ellis's hand and began guiding her towards another room.

"We just need to ask you a couple of questions," the female officer was saying to her too loudly when they broke away from the throng of officers who had practically surrounded her.

Mary Ellis watched as she was swept up by officers into another room. The officer who was still standing next to Mary Ellis, grabbed her shoulder.

"We just need to ask you a couple of questions."

Mary Ellis let herself be led to a small grey room where they did just that. Why didn't you call the police? When did you leave? Did anyone hurt you? Did you hurt anyone? How could you afford to do this? What do you have with you right now? Mary Ellis answered their questions only in the hope that she would never have to come back here.
In the chair, seated across from the large man and woman who were grilling her, she felt like she was five again. Even when they spoke kindly to her and allowed her as much time as she needed to explain what happened, she was shrinking in her seat until she was the same girl that Rachel left behind six years ago. This time there was no family to help her, at least no family that Gran had ever talked about.

When they were finally finished, the female officer who had talked to her originally guided Mary Ellis to the door way and told her they had arranged for Stacy Foster's family to take her in while the searched for any of her living relatives. Then the officer opened the door.

Stacy sat with her father in two of the seats that lined the lobby. She was leaning against the wall, staring at the ceiling. Mary Ellis could imagine what she was thinking. Depending on how long she had been waiting, Stacy might have been playing a game that they always used to play when they were bored: instead of finding shapes in clouds they would look for shapes in the stains or patterns in the ceilings.

Mary Ellis smiled.

"Stacy?" she said quietly.

Stacy's dropped her eyes to look at the voice that was calling her. As she did, a grin spread across her face. She stood up.

"Hi."

Mary Ellis pulled Stacy into a hug. It lingered for a long time, maybe too long, but how nice it was to feel the touch of someone who she truly loved.

"You got famous while you were away. Everyone was worried about you."

"Were they mad at you for not telling?"

The officer was talking in a hushed tone to Stacy's father. Stacy nodded.

"They were pissed." Stacy jerked her head in the direction of her father and Mary Ellis broke into a giggle.

"But you didn't tell my secret."

Stacy looked down at her feet and frowned for a moment.

"What?" Mary Ellis said, a flare of anger rising inside her.

"I was really worried about you. They needed to know where you were."

For a moment, Mary Ellis squeezed her hands into fists. Anger rose insider her. Then, it subsided.

"It's okay. I think I understand."

They stood in silence for a moment. Mary Ellis felt like she was about to cry.

"I'm excited that you get to stay over, even if it's not for forever," Stacy said finally, taking Mary Ellis's hand.

"Me too."

For a moment, Mary Ellis's heart was pricked with fear. She couldn't imagine herself as the girl she had been when she left to find her mother. Though she guessed she looked the same, Mary Ellis's insides had rearranged themselves into something unfamiliar. There were truths she had learned that Stacy couldn't know, didn't need to learn, and Mary Ellis wasn't sure whether that was a good thing or not.

"That's fine, I've been going to the movies a lot," Stacy interrupted her thoughts, a light blush falling over her cheeks, "I figured out how to get there from my house and the way to get there goes right past this bakery that has the most delicious cookies so I like to sneak them in through my sleeves. We can go together."

Mary Ellis grinned.

"And I made a new friend. Leah. We can all hang out together."

***

For the first few days, Stacy's parents wouldn't let Mary Ellis out of their sight. When Stacy asked her parents if they could go to the movies or walk to the playground or even just go out into the circle in center of the cul-de-sac, Stacy's mother and father would offer to take them there and would force them to stay in sight all the time. Stacy constantly complained about this, even letting her conversations with parents devolving into yelling on occasion.

Mary Ellis didn't seem to care though. She would just lounge around on the sofa watching as Stacy got frustrated, nearly laughing.

"Why don't you want to do anything? Why aren't you mad at my parents for lording over us like they don't trust us? It's stupid." Anger marked Stacy's features as she whirled around the room.

"Stacy I just ran away. There was a police investigation." Mary Ellis had a lazy smile on her face. Stacy sank down onto the floor.

"Why are you so casual about this?"

"Because I just missed you. I'm happy to just be around you." Mary Ellis pulled a blanket around her shoulders.

"Maybe we could sneak out, tomorrow. When my mom leaves for brunch we could sneak out the back door while my dad is in the kitchen." Stacy nearly fell into her revolving desk chair and leaned down hard on her desk.

"Why don't you just give your parents a chance to chill out?"

"You would have been so into this a couple of weeks ago." Stacy sighed.

"Let's just watch a movie or something."

Stacy fiddled with a book she had sitting open on her desk.

"Why don't you want to do something interesting? I've been going out all summer just imagining what you would do if we were together, but this isn't what I imagined at all. You're not the Mary Ellis I remembered."

"You're not the same Stacy from before, either, but that doesn't mean anything needs to change. We just need to give your parents a little time to get adjusted to the idea of me being here, then we can start going out again like we used to."

"I just don't want my parents to walk all over us. I don't want to-"

Mary Ellis laughed and sank back onto the sofa. She knew that this is what her life was supposed to be. No matter what happened, Stacy would be there for her and her parents could help to fix whatever problems arose. Mary Ellis was surrounded by people she could trust now, truly. Greater than Gran and certainly greater than Rachel and her father, whoever he was. Mary Ellis had everything she could ever want. Whatever the future could hold, for once Mary Ellis felt ready.

Acknowledgments

If you'd have asked me even a year ago whether I could have dreamed this book would be completed, I would have laughed. I never thought that I'd be able to write something like this, and I wouldn't have been able to without the help of my amazing family and friends. I'd especially like to thank the following people.

Ms. Supplee and Ms. Mlinek thank you so much for supporting my writing even when I believed that it was trash. Ms. Supplee, thank you for taking the time to read and reread my manuscript and for always taking the time to provide the critiques that let the project get to the place it is today. Thank you for providing the original inspiration for this piece. So much of my confidence as a writer comes from things that I have learned from you. Ms. Mlinek, thank you for encouraging me to reach farther with my writing and try things I would have never dreamed of trying before. Thank you for showing me, when I was just a tiny, terrified freshman, that the community that awaited me at Carver was unlike any other and that it would embrace me with open arms.

To the 2019 Literary Arts Class thank you for all of the work that you had to put into this piece as well. Through the revisions the critiques, the cover art feedback, and the endless book pitching, you all have always been there to support me and provide me with invaluable feedback that shaped my book into what it is today. From the first time you all hugged me as I sobbed, after reading my first piece in front of the class, I knew that this experience would be something special and it was because of all of you.

Mom, Dad, and Ruari thank you so much and I'm so so sorry. Without your love and support I would not have made it through the copious number of midnight mental breakdowns and last-minute editing sessions. Though I never let you read anything that I wrote, this piece would not have been the same without you all being there to cheer me on. Mom and Dad, thank you for fostering my love of reading and writing from such a young age, providing me with the foundation I needed to one day reach the place where I currently am.

Lastly, I'd like to thank Emma, Kayla, Aidan, Nicole, and Katie. When I entered the Literary Arts program at Carver, I was so scared that I would lose you and the friendship that you've given me for such a long time. I cannot thank you enough for sticking by me and providing encouragement even when I refused to show you anything I was working on and generally acted insane. More than you all may realize, you have inspired events and locations not only within this story but within everything that I write. I love you all.

Micheline Collins is a senior in G.W. Carver's Literary Arts program. She lives with her parents, sister, cat, Big Tuna, and dog, Nola in Catonsville, MD. Writing has been her passion since she was in elementary school, having started her first newspaper in second grade, which she sold for ten cents outside of her bedroom door. Currently, she has been published in her school's literary magazine, Synergy, which she is now an editor of, and has received multiple Silver Keys in the regional Scholastic Arts and Writing competition for her poetry and an honorable mention in the Jack London writing competition. Her greatest inspirations are authors Philip K. Dick and Rita Mae Brown, who are able to weave worlds out of single ideas and utterly envelope their readers, which Micheline hopes to one day accomplish with her own work.

43887737R00139